I0457999

The Traveler

Sol Smith

Part I: The Hedgewitch
Part II: Traveler
Part III: The Burning Witch

We are not human beings on a spiritual journey, we are spiritual beings on a human journey.
    —*The Pagan Outlook* mission statement.

Part I: The Hedgewitch

One

The carpet is beige. The chairs are a darker beige. The typing, gabbing, and phone calling from all the secretaries sounds *beige*.

"What are you in for this time, honey?" Mary, the secretary who is several years past retirement age asks me.

"Disrupting class," I say.

"Again? Haven't you got anything better to do?"

I smile to recognize the polite humor, but I really think this is a good question. Don't I have something better to do?

"He'll be right with you," she says.

Waiting on the hard plastic chair outside my guidance counselor's office has become a weekly ritual. One I don't look forward to. The meetings are perfunctory and frustrating. Why can't I just be sent to stand in a corner or pick up trash or something? Why does everything have to be so damn serious?

"Uh oh, Abbie." Mary is typing up some kind of report about my arrival to the office. "This is conference number four. You know what that means."

I collapse in my chair. It's going to be a long wait

before my dad gets here.

The door to the office opens slightly and I see Erica's eyes framed by her black hair peering through.

"What, again?"

"Just come in and talk." I pat the plastic seat next to me.

"I've got math class. I think there's a quiz today." She's using a stage whisper, like no one noticed that I've started talking to the cracked door.

"Just sit down for a minute." I try not to whine.

Erica slinks in and sits down next to me. "How many does this make?"

"Four."

"Man. Are they calling your dad?"

"I think they already did."

"He'll be pleased. What class did you act-out in this time?"

"History. This is the second time for history this semester."

"Can't you just sit there and not listen? Can't you just pretend to be somewhere else?"

"No, Erica, I can't. This is important. This is our minds being polluted. I can't just sit there and listen to it all."

"What was it? You have some beef with the signing of the Magna Carta?"

I heave a breath. "Salem."

The word wipes the smile off of Erica's face. She leans back in her chair. "I don't know what your issue is with Salem, Abbie, honestly," she says. "I don't really see how that all is related to who *we* are."

"It's a validation issue, Erica. Get with it."

We're interrupted by Mary leaning over her desk. "Girls, you need to keep it down. And Erica, were you sent here?"

"No ma'am. I was just leaving." She picks up her bag and moves to her feet. "Are you coming to the party?"

"I doubt it. What party?"

"The Halloween party at Mark Hill's place."

"Like I'm going to a Halloween party, Erica, come on."

"Vic will be there," she smiles.

"Please, please don't talk about him, okay? I just want to forget about it all right now, you know?"

"Girls, please," Mary reminds us.

"Sorry," Erica says. "I'm leaving." Then she turns around one more time. "Hey, I found an apartment. I'm getting out of my aunt's house next week. Can you help get some furniture for it this weekend?"

"Maybe, if my dad doesn't kill me. How are you planning on paying for that place, anyway?"

"Mom and Dad. Berkley pays a lot more than Ashlan State, Abbie. They think it'll be good for me. Maybe you can be such a pain in the ass that your dad will kick you out, then you could move in, too."

"Cool. I'll set the curtains on fire when I get home."

"And drink all the milk straight from the bottle. That should do it."

"Abigail," Mary says. "Do you mind not having so much fun when you're being disciplined?"

Erica closes the door behind her, only to reopen it a second later. "Your dad's here," she says.

"Thanks for killing the suspense."

I'm getting to know Mr. Taft's office pretty well. The way it smells like a musty closet; the way the motivational posters hang just a little off balance on every wall; the way his wife and twin sons shine their happy faces through a silver picture frame. The chairs in his office are just a bit more comfortable than in the waiting room, equipped with a layer of padding from 1983 or so. Looking around his office, the only real difference between this visit and my previous visits there is that my dad's sitting next to me.

"It's not a matter of who's right or wrong, Abbie," Dad says after listening to Mr. Taft's side of the story. "It's about respect for the teacher."

"Dad," I say patiently. "It's not like I can just respect someone who asks the class to believe a load of shit like that." My response, and perhaps that one word in particular, seems to have a physical affect on my dad and Mr. Taft.

"Abigail, Mr. Richer is an expert in history. Just like we talked about last week, how Mrs. Oltorf is an expert in physics."

"Oh god, don't get me started on her again."

"Abbie," my dad says. "This is very serious. Please take this seriously." Dad has that look in his eyes, looking through the tops of his eyes. That same look that he would give me when I'd have a friend sleep over, and we were being too loud too late in the night.

I try to explain it to them. I try to explain how every October, some class ends up discussing Salem and the witch hunt. Sometimes it's an English class, sometimes it's a history class, but every year some teacher decides to "educate" the students about witches. This time it was Mr. Richer.

He talked about the hearings. The swimming of the suspects. The hanging of the condemned. The tragic circumstance brought on by ignorance and fear.

"Of course, most witch lore comes from age and class discrimination," Mr. Richer told the class. "Something happens that can't be explained, and they blame it on someone who fits the classic description. The witch hunts really represent the xenophobia and paranoia of a society immersed in ignorant superstition. The idea of the witch was a convenient scapegoat for so many of the society's shortcomings."

And what he's doing there is striking down thousands of years of tradition. He may be right about xenophobia and paranoia and all of that, but he's telling the class—right before my eyes—that the very idea of a witch is concocted from the same material as dragons and unicorns. He's planting the idea that it's all just an old wives' tale or something. Like witches don't matter.

In many ways, this type of education is *worse* than a witch hunt. At least witch hunts verify the existence of a counter belief system. And how can Dad sit here in this office and act like that's not important? I really worry about how much he's changed sometimes.

"And I let him have it," I tell my dad in the counselor's office. "I told him what he was doing, how he was striking down a way of life, a religion thousands of years older than the dominant ones of today with a simple lesson about paranoia meant to serve as a Halloween story."

"And how did the other students react to this?" Mr. Taft says.

I guess his point is that the other students didn't appreciate my passionate interruption. Like they were there to learn and I was ruining it for everyone or something.

"They laughed," I say. "For whatever reason, speaking your mind in class always seems laughable. Mr. Richer got mad, and I said a few more things that I guess were disrespectful, and there was more laughter. And finally they called me a witch, like that was supposed to be a bad thing, and there was more laughing, and there was more yelling on Mr. Richer's part. You know how these things go. A dead end."

"A dead end," says Mr. Taft. "So, what did you feel like you gained from this?"

I think about the question for a second. They both look at me like there's some kind of lesson here that I should be receptive to. They look at me with expectation, like I'm going to come to some kind of realization that being laughed at made the whole thing not worth it.

"I learned that I should speak my mind no matter

what the consequence."

By the looks of their falling faces, I learned the wrong lesson.

Two

I cut up rose petals and put them in an infuser. Next I add thyme, yarrow, cinnamon, and cloves. It smells sweet, musty, with a full floral body. I lock the infuser tight and put it in the boiling water.

The water that I am using is full moon water. It sat outside my window in a clear jar all night, soaking in the light of the full moon. I don't always use full moon water, but I try to make some every month for use in something. It was something that Mom, Dad and I used to do together. It was the mark that another month had passed when we would gather our jars from the kitchen and fill them with water to set outside for the long night.

Like they said in class, I am a witch. But don't jump to whatever conclusion you were about to make. When I was younger, Dad taught me that there are at least 17 different meanings for the word *witch*. Saying I'm a witch is an unspecific description. So if you're disgusted, if you're intrigued, afraid, mad—it says more about you than it does about me. You can learn a lot about someone's upbringing, their preconceptions, and their vocabulary by their reaction to the word *witch*.

When I say I'm a witch, I don't mean that I'm

goth. I don't mean that I wear purple lipstick against pale skin. I don't wear black lace and my fingernails aren't pierced.

I'm not a heretic, either, and I don't worship Satan—two Biblical interpretations. To be a heretic or a Satanist means that you do in fact adhere to Christian dogma. I don't.

The tea has to boil for 10 minutes, forcing me to listen to Dad and Teri talk in the other room. They are listening to *Some Kind of Blue* and drinking some kind of red wine that they've been into lately. They talk softly, painting murmurs over the sound of the boiling water. Dad doesn't mention the unpleasant business at school to Teri. I think he wants her to believe that I'm still a good student. He thinks that will help us get along through this whole transition.

The tea doesn't taste great, but I don't cut it with cream or milk. I never cut it with cream or milk because they just aren't part of the tea. Besides, I remember Mom telling me, it would just make more of it that I'd have to drink.

When mom was alive, we recognized Samhain as a family. We'd carve pumpkins and light them and decorate the whole house with them. We'd set up empty chairs with black plates and black candles lit on them and sit to eat a feast of mostly homegrown food. It was always a quiet, happy banquet with the loved ones we invited who had passed.

We kept the tradition for a few years after Mom

died. Dad and I would do all the decorating together. We'd hold hands at the table, inviting Mom to join us, sit right between us. He never shed a tear at those Samhains.

I don't know if the medications kicked in or what, but all of a sudden one year he just stopped caring .Or, he stopped pretending to care. Now he just doesn't seem to think about Samhain. Or Wicca.

My mother was a witch. She was beautiful. She was stunning. I've heard more than one person describe her as *bewitching*. You can also use *witch* to call someone a hag.

I don't know if I'm bewitching. But I'm not a hag, either.

Back in my room, I sip my tea as I draw my circle for the banishing ritual. I set up candles at the four cardinal points. I ask The Lady to be with me tonight, to protect me within my circle. I ask the forces all around me to help, to lend me their knowledge, teach me, help me grow, connect, become one. I draw the circle with my dagger; white handle, silver blade, and a cherub carved into the hilt. It was my mother's dagger. And her mother's. We don't know, really, how far back it goes. But Mom once said it was hundreds of years old.

Outside the circle, I light incense. Incense has been used by more than Wiccans. Hindus, Buddhists, Catholics, and countless other belief systems use incense ceremoniously.   The scent of the incense cleanses the air, keeps impurities out of the system. It wards off spirits. Awakens inner parts of you.

I'm not a magician. And I don't have a wide-brimmed conical hat. I hate cats.

I know herbs, but I'm not a witchdoctor. I don't practice voodoo or hoodoo or Santeria. I'm not a Celtic Druid. Or Asatru.

I made the incense using Dad's old formula two days ago by grinding rosemary, cinnamon sticks, makko and sandalwood. I added sage and frankincense that I had bought from a shop down the street and mixed it all with water—river water—and made a paste. The paste I rolled into cones and then set on a window sill in the sun to dry. Dad used to spend Friday nights making incense. I still can't get it quite as good as he does.

In Exodus 22:18, they describe a witch as an evil sorcerer. I'm not a sorcerer. I'm not a wizard in a fantasy book. I'm not Harry Potter.

I call myself a witch, and I don't mean that I dowse for water.

Dad's incense is to help with the meditation. To take me deeper within myself. His specialty was meditation. And yet even that couldn't get him out of the depression that he was in.

Mom's tea is to help with the projection. She never told me where she got the recipe, but it's not in our family's grimmerie. She was great at projection, better than her mother ever was. And she taught me everything that she knew before I was 10.

But there are other parts to my solitary Samhain ceremony. I write five words on a strip of paper:

Depression.

Resentment.

Weakness.

Pain.

Fear.

Each word is representative of something I want to get rid of in my life. Each one is something that troubled me the previous year. It is a banishing list. Sort of like a reverse resolution.

The list has to be dipped in alcohol and then dropped in a black iron bowl in the center of my circle. I light the list and in a flash, the words are gone. I let this image resonate within me, hoping to banish them thoroughly.

Witch can be used as a general slur, a substitute for *bitch*. I can be one of those, I guess, but that's not what I mean.

I sit down within my circle, comfortable, at home. I can feel the energy this Samhain is right. I can feel my body agree with the night. I make another list, but this one is just in my head. I humbly ask for growth in my arts. I ask for growth in my music. I ask for self-discipline and focus in my personal life.

I don't do banishments at the end of the Wiccan

year because I have been told to. I don't make resolutions because it is tradition. I feel the need to renew in my blood. I feel the need to move on in my bones. I know this in the same way the trees know this. The same way the rabbits know this. The same way the sun knows this.

When I say I'm a witch, I don't mean that I was born with supernatural powers. In fact, I don't think there's anything supernatural about my practice of witchcraft. The idea of my witchcraft is to be close to nature. To establish rhythm and harmony between me and the natural world.

I've heard it called Neo-paganism. Or Earth-Centered religion. Or Animism. I'd even say that some of the connotations of the term *white majick* aren't far off.

I come from a long line of witches; women who passed their beliefs, their practices, down from mother to daughter for more generations than we are aware of. It isn't done coldly, without meaning. It is part of me. It is inherent to who I am. I must do it. I am driven to. It's a beautiful thing, a beautiful way of life. And I suppose that's the reason I get so upset when it is trivialized. That's why I get angry when a teacher tells a class that there never were any witches in the first place.

It just doesn't seem fair. It's heartless, really, to say something like that.

I sit in the middle of the circle. The tea, I remember, is to help with the projection. I already feel light and tingly.

We are solitary practitioners; hedgewitches. My mom met with a coven a couple of times, but found it to be too shallow and ritualistic. No, our relationship is with The Lady, Earth, Nature—not with other witches. But still, I know there are others. I respect others.

But I'm the last of my line. My mother died when I was 12. We've been in contact since then—I am a witch, after all.

While we have a family Book of Shadows, we adhere to no other scripture, books, or documents. A Bible can be torn. A Koran can decay. The Vedas can burn.

Our bible or scriptures are the wind, the rain, the trees, the moon. The stars guide us. The seasons ebb and flow in our blood. So maybe that is why it is so easy to discount us. We don't attract attention, when we can help it. I guess that we learned that lesson the hard way.

Now it's time for the part of the ceremony that I look forward to all year long. I have a simple wooden flute that took me all summer to carve. I play a single note—solid and unwavering at first, then a slight vibrato. The candle light flickers with the vibrato. I feel the note in my core. I resonate with the note.

Then, when I can totally feel the note in every fiber of my body, I lower the note.

The candle light lowers. My body's vibration lowers.

And again.

And again.

I breathe in the smell of frankincense; dark, musty, smoky.

I taste the rose petals and cinnamon.

And when the vibrations are low enough, and the candles are low enough, I step out of my body and look around.

Three

I remember my first out of body experience. I was ten and staying home sick from school with the chicken pox. My mom had drawn a bath for me and added salts *(three parts geranium, one part frankincense, one part rosemary—she never did anything without telling me exactly how she did it)* to cleanse and relax my body.

She had run to the store and I stayed in my bath, periodically warming it up and adding more salts. I was relaxed until near sleeping when I heard my mom's car. At the time, I wasn't great at the meditation stuff, but I knew, at least on an intellectual level, what it was all about. Mom had gone over what projection was, and Dad was teaching meditation workshops in the living room on the weekends. So maybe it had all sunk in all of a sudden and that's why, without thinking, I found myself standing naked in the driveway watching my mom's car pull in. I was embarrassed beyond belief.

My mom got out of the car and grabbed a bag of groceries. She didn't notice, which was more relaxing than disturbing. I followed her into the house and watched in awe as she called out to me.

"I'm home," she said, and walked down the hall

to the bathroom.

I followed and was getting panicked, as she still couldn't see me. Standing in the doorway behind my mom, I saw myself lying in the steaming hot bath. I wasn't afraid I was dead, because I didn't recognize myself immediately.

We are not used to seeing our bodies in three dimensions. It is an alien experience to us. I stood there wondering who it was in the bathtub, and I was suddenly incredibly close to my own sleeping face.

I awoke with a start, pulled quickly back into my body as my mom touched my arm. The itching chicken pox were a welcome feeling.

As I stare at my body this Samhain night, I am no less astounded by what I look like from the outside. Somehow, I can be less critical from outside of it. Somehow, I look just like a girl I would pass on the street. Somehow, I have compassion for the person that I'm looking at.

Overall, there's a certain prettiness about me that I don't usually see in myself. And I can chalk this up to a couple of different things. First, I've noticed that while you are spending time out of your body, petty insecurities and self-criticisms are left in the body; it's just like deep meditation, where you learn that your thoughts are not you. And secondly, I'm not photogenic. I don't look good in a two-dimensional, head-on, squashed flat vantage point. But I seem to look fine from all around.

I think that we tend to think of ourselves in some

kind of a portrait way. Most pictures that we see of ourselves are taken bust-line up from the front. We look into mirrors in the same way. We keep thinking that this picture is what we look like, while everyone else is isn't locked into a frame in our minds.

The world is richer than the pictures I think I look like. But I don't see the other people in my life this way. When I picture my mom, I see her from an angle below her, looking up. I see her cutting vegetables in the kitchen in full motion, while I tug at her long flowing skirt. She smiles, white teeth under pink lips. The sunlight comes through the window, changing and washing over her face in the gentle sway of the tree branches.

Or I picture her picking those vegetables from the garden. On her knees, dirt on her face, she reaches into the earth and pulls up her carrots. Her long fingers burrow holes in the soil, showing me how to replant.

Or I picture her playing cello. I'm crouched low on a hardwood floor in our living room. She's playing a slow, strong song that I feel vibrating in the floor beneath me. Her eyes are closed, her face oscillates between a contort of pain and a soft sigh of comfort and relief, as does the music.

Pictures don't capture this. Mirrors squash it flat under their glass feet.

I picture my dad teaching a workshop in our house. He speaks quietly, but his voice carries over the wooden floors and around the walls. He talks the same way in the classes that I used to watch him teach at the college when I was little, pacing back and forth in front of a chalkboard.

I picture my dad lying on the couch. He's crying out in pain, like a child shoved into a grown man's body. He begs me to find his pills in the kitchen. To pour him water. To sit with him. His rough hands hold mine. His eyes pinch out tears.

This was after Mom died. And no picture could show you the difference that I could feel in him when the medicine finally took hold.

I picture Vic with curls of smoke leaving his mouth as he looks over his shoulder, sullenly, at a coffee shop. And I try not to picture him naked, lit by candlelight.

I picture Erica with a half-smile sneaking across her down-turned face. I picture her legs flexing under her skirt as she walks. I can see those same legs kicking and stomping on her bed when I shoved a needle through her nose. And I can see her smile from 180 separate degrees as she looks in the mirror gazing at her nose's new diamond stud.

I picture Teri laughing on that same couch where Dad was crying, holding some fragrant glass of wine. Her upper lip pulls back so far that her gums are exposed when she laughs. She throws her head back and I can see every tendon and blood vessel in her elongated neck.

But we don't see ourselves this elastically. We see ourselves as solid, unchanging people; tepid snapshots of dull and pallid lives.

Everyone should try this. Everyone should step out of their bodies and see the shell left behind as everyone else does. Everyone should see how real and solid they actually are. It should be an experience that we all go through—part of growing up, part of being a person. You have a more genuine respect for yourself after you've viewed your body this way. You take yourself more seriously as a functional person.

I finish ogling myself and turn to the window. It's not quite a full moon, but I feel its pull strongly. Invigorated by the sensation, in my astral body, I run and leap into the pecan tree in our backyard.

Somewhere in the air, I have lost my body's form and look more like the shadow of a cat—if anyone could see me. I have no definite edges or form; I change quickly like fast-motion smoke, only my center staying whole.

I crawl and leap from branch to branch, tree to tree, feeling charged by the energy of the trees and of the moon above. An ecstatic joy builds up inside me, pulsing kinetic energy that builds rather than dissipates with my movements.

I run and jump for I don't know how long. If it's for five minutes or for the whole night, I wouldn't be surprised.

Energy transference from the natural world. I have practiced this method for about a year. My great-grandmother wrote extensively about the practice of it in our Book of Shadows. It is a way to commune with Nature. A way to build intent. A way to renew your energy and feel refreshed for days to come. A great way to start the new year.

I find myself blocks away from home, almost to the main drag near Mission Square before I decide to go back. And waiting on the back lawn under my window is Mom. Just like every Samhain for the past six years.

Four

"Mom," I call to her as I come down the oak in our backyard, gaining my human form.

"Happy New Year, Abbie," she calls back.

I always see my mom the same way since she died—beautiful and in her prime, how she looked when I was 10 years old. I never saw her as the woman who was dying in a hospital bed when I was 12. Dying of a rare degenerative brain condition that was never satisfactorily diagnosed. And god, how she hated hospitals. Maybe that was one of the reasons that she was a midwife.

"Abbie, you looked so beautiful up there, running like that."

"I didn't know you were here already, I wouldn't have kept you waiting."

"You've learned a lot and are progressing so well, Abbie. I'm very proud of you. And to think you are doing so well without me there to help you."

While I've never wanted to be a midwife, I have always respected the role that my mom wanted to play in women's lives. She wanted to be there for them during their most precious moments, to make sure that they were fully present at the birth of their children. It was a holy thing for my mother, to be there at the arrival of new life. She didn't feel like a hospital was the right place for that.

I don't know how I feel about that. I think I might run into a hospital with my shirt lifted up asking for the needle in the waiting room.

Mom and I sit under the stars which shine very bright to your eyes when you're projecting. Though I suppose we might not need it, we sit on the wrought iron bench that surrounds the oldest oak in our yard. We rarely leave the yard when we meet, which is only two or three times a year.

Tonight we talk about a lot. I think Mom can see that I'm feeling splintered. She even mentions my sleeping with Vic, which embarrasses me to no end.

"It's okay, dear," she assures me. "It's normal to feel lost at times. It's normal to act out. It's normal to feel like a singularity. You should really consider talking to Dad more about his kind of thing."

"He's been busy lately. I talked to him more in the counselor's office the other day than I had in months." Suddenly I felt colder. I don't want to talk to Mom about all this stuff. I want to bury my head in her chest and sob for a while. But I just stay kind of silent.

"Your dad's girlfriend is moving in, isn't she?" Mom asks, without it sounding like a complaint or a judgment.

"I'm sorry, Mom."

"No, don't be. I think she's okay, and it's so great

to see your dad this happy again."

"I know Mom, but I just feel so weird about the whole thing."

"No, no. Don't worry. My feelings aren't hurt."

"Mine are. I don't know. I just can't sleep at night lately, thinking of her being in the other room."

"Can't sleep?" my mother says incredulously. "You know how to fix that, dear. Don't act like a child when you're not one."

My mother was a thousand times better with herbs than I am. She followed our family's long tradition of herbal medicine, potions, and spells. I've picked a lot of it up, but I also rely on all the meditation practices that my dad taught me.

"I was thinking," Mom continues, "your dad probably won't be using my old bed anymore."

"He moved out of the guest room a couple months ago, right before he started dating Teri."

"I know it's overly large for your room, but it's such a beautiful and inspiring piece of furniture. It could be a small gesture of change in your life."

Mom always talked to me about *gestures*. She taught me that if you want to instigate a change in your life, you change something—a practice, a habit, a room arrangement—and always remember why you made that change. It's an outward symbol to the universe that you are changing.

"Maybe with my bed, you'll soak up a little more of my energies. Your practices may improve. Take out our Book and see what it says about changing the path of your life. You're growing up, Abigail. This is a very holy and wonderful time in your life. You look just like a *lady* sitting here before me. I wish I could have seen this with my own eyes. You are so *beautiful*."

Mom always had such a wonderful and positive view of life. That probably also led her to go into the work that she did. Being a midwife came easily to my mom. She grew up around other people's births. My grandmother would take her along to births and have her assist from a very young age.

She grew up in the coastal town of Pacific Grove and attended births in Monterey, Salinas, Big Sur, and Carmel. But even with her familiarity, births never became commonplace to her. She never lost her sense of awe that she experienced at every birth, she told me once when she was still alive. When I was born, however, she had to have a cesarean.

It was a cruel joke, in her mind, that she couldn't give natural birth. The rushed operation damaged my mother, rendering her uterus a hostile environment and preventing any future pregnancies. After helping countless women give natural birth, she was never able to experience it herself. She was unconscious during the procedure, having lost a great deal of blood. She didn't see me until I was an hour old. And I always wonder if there isn't a small part of her that feels that was her 'burning at the stake'; God punishing her for easing Eve's Pains.

"I just don't know Mom," I say about nothing in particular. "I wish I could just stay here with you." I look up at the stars—they don't seem so distant when you're out of your body.

"Don't even joke about it, honey," Mom says. "Life is a sacred gift. Take it as yours. Make it your own."

I sigh. I hold her hand and bury my face in her neck. I almost feel like I can *smell* her.

Samhain is my favorite night of the year. It always has been. The veil between worlds is at its thinnest, allowing us to easily travel in and out of boundaries. But tonight, sitting with my mom and looking at the stars, it may be my favorite night ever. She died before I was old enough to question her. And now that she's gone, I'm still trying to be just like her. I suppose I'm stuck here, in arrested development, thinking the whole world of her. Wishing I could be her.

Five

I love the view from my bedroom window. Directly under it is the roof of the back porch. It's a perfect stoop for sitting on clear nights. I grow many of my herbs in planters on this "balcony." Our yard is filled with oaks and pecan trees, one of which towers over our house. The branches of this tree are just out of reach from my rooftop stoop, but they filter light perfectly, day and night.

Because of the flourishing branches, I took the blinds off my window long ago. On clear nights with a full moon, the light pours through the tree and paints patterns on the floor and walls of my room. The wind brushes the blue and black figures around the room, and it gives the visual illusion of washing in a gentle tide.

My bedroom is awash in this oak filtered moonlight tonight, and I squeeze to the side of Mom's over-sized bed, half sleeping and watching the movement of the silhouettes on the walls. There is a familiar feeling sleeping in this bed again. Beyond the physical recognition, there's a mental comfort that makes me feel at home. I have the overwhelming feeling that I'm not alone in the bed; I'm cushioned all around by an energy that makes me feel like I'm a child in my mother's arms again. Yet the energy isn't that of my mother's; I know what my mother feels like, and this is not her.

Still, I think as I start to drift off, there's something here that makes me feel at home. It's a disarming feeling; a feeling that lets me relax fully. I hear my breathing slow down, and fall to sleep.

Vic and I sit on the outside patio of the Café Andante. I am excited to be wearing a jacket on this cold November night. The weather has been unseasonably warm the last few weeks, and I feel so cozy and attractive when I'm bundled up. Vic sat down and I felt myself touch my hair. I had been feeling my hair all day. For the past 17 years, my fingers have known my hair to be blond. It somehow felt different being black.

I woke up a few days before and wanted to dye it. I'm not sure why. Something in me was begging for a change. I looked in the mirror for a while, and tried and tried to picture myself with black hair.

The dye was tricky. I knew that you can use sage to darken your hair, but it takes weeks and weeks to do so. I went with the more extreme measure. I crushed walnut shells boiled them for three hours. I removed the hulls and strained them so I was left with the water. I let the water boil longer until it had diminished quite a bit so I was left with a thick dark liquid. I added a pinch of cloves and let it sit in the out on my balcony overnight. Then, this morning, I rinsed it through my hair time and time again, and let it sit in it for an hour before finally washing it out. The result was a very dark black color.

And I'm hoping that I'll be able to get the dye out of the tub.

"I haven't seen you around for a while," Vic says. "When did you go black?" He takes a long, careful drag from his cigarette. He's been smoking since he was 14 or so. He started because it makes you look cool. I think if he could quit he wouldn't, for the very same reason.

"I don't know," I say. "It's been a while."

The black hair looks good. I feel more confident with it. I feel somehow like people will see me with new eyes. Like they will treat me like someone else.

"How was your Halloween? Or *Dia de los Muertos¸* or whatever you people call it?" Vic is one of the few people who knows I'm a witch; that I'm *really* a witch. He finds it a great source of fun.

"Samhain," I say. "And it was very good. And whose fault is it that we haven't seen each other lately?"

"You could come to one of my shows, you know," Vic says. "You know where I play on Thursday nights."

"And I know that it costs seven bucks to get in, too."

"Damn worth it, too," and here is another carefully placed drag on his cigarette. It would seem uncontrived if it weren't so totally nonchalant. "Erica was there."

"You've been spending some time with her, huh?"

"She's been around."

"God, I'm sorry I ever introduced you two. Really, you're both totally sprung on each other and way too cool to do anything about it."

"She's good looking," Vic says indifferently.

Vic has always been a good friend to me. But a few months ago, in a moment of either intense passion or extreme boredom, well, something happened. And I guess that I took it differently than he did. I suppose I got the wrong idea about things, but his attitude that it was just a night between friends has really put a burden on our friendship.

On Samhain, one of the words I wrote down on the banishing list was *weakness*. Vic was that weakness; or, rather, my weakness was in giving myself to him. I undervalued myself, not asking for anything in return. Now I dread lulls in conversation with him. I dread the things I think in the void.

"My mom had this bed ever since she was little," I tell him eagerly, not letting the conversation drop off. "It's a sleigh bed, very old and very elaborately carved."

"The angel bed, right? The one in the guest room."

"Right. I used to use it when I was little. I thought it was so pretty and that the angels would protect me when I slept in it."

"Protect you from what? Ghosts and *witches* and the like?"

"Ha, ha," I snicker back. "It was a really big bed for a little girl like I was. So I had this imaginary friend—a big sister—who I would pretend shared the bed with me. Her name was Traveler."

Vic laughs. "Where did you get that name?"

"I'm not sure. I guess she told me that was her name," I say lamely.

"So whose imagination was it that made her your friend?"

"Again, Vic, you're just funny as hell."

"Fine, fine, go on with your story. Why are you thinking about the bed and the friend now?"

"I started sleeping in the bed again."

"You took it out of the guest room?"

"I stopped sleeping in the bed when I was eight. My grandma came and stayed with us for a while. So we moved it in there for her."

"Grandma Ruth, right? The crazy one?"

"You remember her?"

"How could I forget? She was totally batty, wasn't she? Scary."

"She ended up that way. That's kind of how I remember her now." I think about Grandma Ruth, about how the days before she died she kept rambling on about a gypsy who was after her. About how this gypsy was going to cast a spell on her and how I should stay away from gypsies. We tried to get her not to say that word, my mom and I. But it was like she was beyond learning, and didn't care that she was sounding so racist.

"The bed," I say, "just kind of stayed in that room. My mom slept on it when she got sick. And my dad slept on it after she died."

"But now there's Teri," Vic said, showing that he was not only listening, but following along.

"Now there's Teri, and Dad has gone back into his bedroom. So I took the bed back."

"And let me guess, Traveler is still in it." Vic opened his eyes wide in an expression of mock fright.

"There wasn't anything scary about Traveler, ass. But I was thinking that my grandma and my mom died in that bed."

"Yuck."

"Exactly. I mean, it's an old bed. Who knows how many people die in old beds like this?"

"Maybe it has a taste for witch blood," he says.

I see it register on his face how tasteless this remark was. I give him a look, and he nods a "sorry." I let it drop.

"I sleep on a futon from Wal-Mart," he says. "That way I know that nothing disagreeable has ever happened on it." Vic takes another one of his long drags on his cigarette. I watch as the curls of smoke twist and spin in their air currents until they dissipate into nothing. The dissipation reminds me of how I feel when I project—like I turn into smoke.

"It just makes me sad to think about it," I say. "I hate to be reminded that Mom died."

Vic shakes his head. "You don't need to be reminded, Abbie."

We sit here for a while longer, him smoking and me people-watching. These silences used to be fine between us. He used to be comfortable and somehow sweet. We'd been around each other so long that talking wasn't needed for communication; the company was what mattered.

For Christ's sake, my mom delivered him. I was eight months old at the time. It was Mom's first delivery since having me and she brought me along. We'd been friends for so long that I was actually in the room when he was born.

But now it's different. Now when we're not talking, we not talk about *something*. We're not talking about the sex. Every moment of silence between us, my mind races to the fact that he has seen me naked. That he has touched and felt parts of my skin that no one else in the world has ever been allowed to see. Is he thinking about it now? When it's quiet, what part of my body is he touching?

"Come on out on Thursday." His voice shatters the silence and I am clothed again. "I'll put you on the list."

"List?"

"We can each get one person in free."

"You never told me this before?"

"I've been letting my brother in."

"Isn't he a little young to be there?"

"He can take care of himself."

"Really, Vic. Don't corrupt the poor guy." For some reason I always see Derek, Vic's little brother, as something more holy than Vic. He seemed like he was pure and innocent, kind and considerate. Or maybe I just put that image onto him because I need someone to be that way.

"I'll put you on next week. Derek will be fine."

"What an honor," I say with mock dignity.

A long careful drag. "No biggie." And a slow release of smoke.

Six

November is a terrible time to troll garage sales. Not so bad as December, but light years away from April or May. Nevertheless, I pick up my dad's paper from the coffee table and start to pick my way through some kind of route for the day. The advertised garage sales aren't always the best, but they provide good points A and B when the real finds can be in one of the innumerable points C along the way.

A few weeks ago, when garage sale season wasn't quite so dead, I had two major finds. While there was nothing of interest at the sale listed as *"Estate sale: furniture and lawn care items"* on Barstow, I found a 1947 Gibson mandolin down the street at a smaller sale; I don't play, but it's gorgeous. I stopped at a sale on Sunset while I was on my way to *"Baby items and clothes"* on Vartikian, and found a stack of LPs that had everything from Chopin to Gordon Lightfoot.

I bought the records—22 in all—for five bucks. I bought the mandolin, worth just under a thousand dollars, for 25. I don't play mandolin, but it has the same fingerings as violin, which I have been playing since I was six.

Today I mark *"Moving Sale"* on Franklin and

"Cribs, couches, and more" on Veranda. I never know exactly what I'm looking for when I head out the door, but there are some items that always catch my eye. Musical instruments are a given. My dad has a kick-ass stereo system complete with a turn-table, so I'm always looking for LPs too. I mean, the invention of the CD was the best thing to ever happen to a vinyl fan who's willing to spend their weekends trolling through people's unwanted things. Sheet music is a rare find. Good books are probably harder to find in yard sales.

Vases, though. I love vases. I talked my dad into letting me have an entire cabinet in the kitchen for my vases alone. We have an old house - one of the oldest in Ashlan - and while its very large, it has a stupidly small amount of storage space. I had to shuffle things around in the kitchen for an entire weekend just to find a way to get an empty cabinet for myself.

Dad thinks it's a waste of money. I rarely buy flowers and most of the instruments I buy I can't even play. But there's some kind of holiness to these things for me. Something about them goes beyond their form and function. And just to have them around is soothing and enrapturing at once.

I gave Erica a call, and she's going to pick me up this time. She's looking for a bookshelf, and she drives an old Chevy S-10.

She gets to my house quickly and already has coffee waiting for both of us in the car. Whether this is just benign of her or if she's softening me up is not clear. I know Erica well, and I love her very much, but I never could bring myself to trust her totally. I've always held it against myself that this is the case.

"Morning, Abbie," she smiles. "I slept like shit last night. Want some coffee?"

"Maybe you sleep like shit because of all the coffee you drink."

"All I drank yesterday was a bunch of canned water."

Here's where I'm supposed to ask why. I don't, and that doesn't deter her one bit. She continues as if I had taken the bait.

"My parents are moving the last of the stuff out of the basement and Dad's getting rid of his Y2K stockpile."

I laugh in earnest, knowing her dad and the kicks he's been on. Her dad is in the philosophy department with my dad. Her mom was friends with my mom, too. But Erica and I have only been friends for a couple years.

When I was 15, I got kind of lonely in my practice. It was around that time that Dad started taking the meds and was able to go back to work. He totally stopped practicing, and had given up the illusion of practicing. He felt bad about my isolation and suggested a solution to it. Dr. Vega and his wife were Wiccan, and they practiced in a coven that met in the foothills. Dad told me that Dr. Vega and the coven would be happy to have me join, if I wanted to. He had a daughter about my age, he said, who would be happy to take me with her.

They preferred to meet outside, they told me, but we were instead in someone's trailer home because it was pouring in sheets outside. The trailer was on the depressing side of the spectrum and, honestly, may have done as much as anything else to taint my view of the coven.

The furniture in the room was all pushed to the edges and extra folding chairs were brought out— uncomfortable and slippery. There were 20 or so people there, which I was told was a poor turn-out because of the rain. They were all of all ages, from half-interested children to some of the oldest women I've ever seen.

The meeting was run by an older woman, draped in black, who had crystals hanging from every hangable feature of her person. She opened the meeting by leading an invocation to invite The Goddess to join us and bless us with her wisdom.

And they all said it together.

That's what bothered me more than anything else. They all knew what to say and they said it as one. My understanding of the craft is that there was no repetition, no rehearsed sayings. It just felt kind of, well, *wrong* compared to how Mom taught me.

The meeting was formal, but filled with the positive feelings of everyone there. I don't mean to be disparaging because many people get a lot out of practicing in a coven. Just to know that there were so many people that believed similar to me was very comforting and encouraging. But I could tell immediately that *this* coven, at least, was not for me.

Erica drove me back to down into the valley a couple of hours later. We talked in the cab of her truck for the 45 minutes that it took to get down the hill. She said that she had met my mother. That Mom had come to her house several times when Erica was younger to talk to her mother. She said that she could tell my mother was a witch and was fascinated to know that there were witches outside of her coven.

Erica was concentrating on the road, squinting at the rain soaked window, her face lit blue from underneath by the dashboard lighting as she told me this. The lighting and the atmosphere, combined with the fact that she was talking about Mom made me realize what a beautiful girl she was. She had striking coloring—long, jet black hair and pale blue eyes against dark skin. Even when her face relaxed she had a cat-like smile pasted there.

She respected my decision to not join the coven—though she still invites me a few times a year—and we have been good friends ever since. We rarely talk about our practices, but when we do, I get a small rush knowing that I'm speaking to someone who *understands*.

"I saw a sale on the way over that looked totally kick-ass," she says as I shut the door to her truck. "No shelves, but plenty of other stuff. We can check it out on the way to the other ones."

"Cool," I say. I look in my purse to see how much money I have left. 23 bucks. With such a finite amount of money, I have to pace my spending. But it's Sunday, and I get paid tonight, so there's no worry about saving any of it for the rest of the week.

"You playing tonight," she asks on cue.

"As always. On at seven."

"You need to get a real job."

"You need to get real coffee. This tastes like dirt."

"I added a little something to it," Erica says.

"What?" Her smile doesn't reveal anything. "Is it dirt? Because that's what it tastes like. Like you added dirt." She keeps smiling. "Okay, dirt. Cool."

The first three places we go don't offer much. On Holland, an old lady has died and left a collection of potholders for her children to sell. She also left velvet paintings of bullfighters and touch lamps and cookbooks from the '50s. I look through a couple of the books and see five recipes that call for MSG. There's this funny Girl Scout handbook from however many years ago that I almost buy because of the illustrations on the inside, but I think that I shouldn't *try* to waste money.

On Veranda, a couple is selling a baby crib, a changing table, and a newborn car seat. They also have clothes and baby toys. Their toddler runs around getting into trouble which I find comforting; at least they didn't lose a baby, they're just getting rid of the stuff he doesn't need anymore. Which means that he will be an only child, and I find the thought bothersome; I always wanted a sister.

Down the street, also on Veranda, a woman is selling an old bike, and an ugly recliner, and clothes.

We drive by without stopping.

On Franklin, a family is moving. They are selling two couches, a dog house, a collection of fans, a few unfortunate wall hangings, and two twin bed sets. Erica asks if they have any bookcases, and a man and a teenager run inside and come out with a low, long case made of dark wood. Erica jumps up and down clapping her hands. I think she's going to kiss them for a moment, but she stops just short before handing over the bills.

"You should play with Vic sometime," she says when we get back in the car.

"Where? At Stones? God Erica, it's not really my scene, don't you think?"

"He could play an acoustic set with you," she says. "Besides, they're always playing the same stuff. It's getting kind of dull."

"I know. Notice I haven't been coming lately."

"Have you been even once since…" Here she pauses, as if to think of a word that isn't too graphic. "Since *you know*?" she finally settles on.

"Since I know *what*?"

"Since you know, you guys *you know*?"

I thought about it a moment, just to make it look like I had to think about it. "I don't think so. But it's not because of that. I'm just kind of bored of the scene, you know?"

"I think I know. He feels bad, you know Abbie?"

"What the hell?" I say. "You guys talk about it?"

"Oh chill, Abbie. I think it's kind of sweet, right?

46

I mean, it sucks that you're hurt but—"

"It's not cool to talk about me with him, Erica. Who says I'm hurt?"

"You think it doesn't show? Jesus, Abbie, you think no one can tell?"

"Stop. There's one back there. Turn right."

The garage sale is lucky. I don't want to talk about this, not now. It's too, I don't know, broad daylight to sit here and talk about sex and friendship and wounds and shit.

This sale is on Cambridge. Another estate sale. Another person has died without figuring out how to take their stuff with them. All the little things this woman acquired that no one in her family wants are sitting on fold-out tables, being paged through by people she never met.

I don't believe in ghosts. Not in the traditional sense, anyway. True, I talk to Mom, and she watches me, but I also know that what I see and talk to is an expression of her greater, immortal self. She's not attached to her life, or her things, or her earthly desires anymore. She's much more like a Goddess that I see as 'Mom'; an expression of one of the forms that she took while on Earth.

Even so, watching these people shuffle through the small details of this unknown woman's life, I can't help but imagine her ghost standing there angry or embarrassed as people look through her dresses, her dishes, her figurines, and her vases. Suddenly I feel really bad about looking through that Girl Scout handbook and laughing.

There are about a dozen vases for sale. And I have a rule about this. Unless I know that I can turn a profit, I am only allowed to buy one vase per garage sale. It's not fair just to add substantially to my collection by just assimilating someone else's. So Erica and I spend a few minutes weeding the collection down to four choices.

The first is a Peruvian vase, decorated with geometric looking fish swimming around it. It's bigger than any others in my collection, and that bothers me.

There's a small, delicate bud vase made of leaded glass that has Erica's attention. It is slender, tall, and very attractive, but too much like a couple other bud vases that I have.

The third vase is clear glass and disc shaped—large around but slim in profile. I'm at the verge of buying this one too, when Erica tells me that she won't let me—I have to play by the rules.

The vase I buy is a beautiful multi-layered work. It is blown by hand, I can tell. It looks like an emerald green teardrop encased in a clear outer casing. When I look at it, I feel somehow comforted by the bright green sunken in the clear shell. I am softly reminded of sleeping in my mother's bed, being comforted and protected; I'm not sure if it's the form or the color that makes me feel this way.

The sellers see how much I admire the piece and they won't let it go for a penny less than the 20 dollar label on it. I buy it and they say it's probably worth much more. She collected vases, they tell me, from

Italy and Brazil and a dozen other places. They kept the best ones, they say, which leaves me wondering how they could have any better than this.

I wrap the vase in the sweater I brought but that it's too warm to use by now. I hold it on my lap like a baby when we get to the car.

"Good morning, huh?" Erica says.

"Very good."

"Do you mind coming by my apartment?"

"Let me guess," I say. "You need help with the bookshelf."

"Just a little," she says. "Just to get it up the stairs. You don't need to put books on it or anything tedious like that."

"That's good," I say. "I'd hate to get stuck lifting books all day long, you know?"

Erica lives in an apartment. Her parents moved away last summer when her dad got a job at a college in the Bay Area. They haven't sold the house, and I don't know why Erica doesn't just live there. She is a year older than I am and she graduates this year. After begging and pleading, her parents let her stay in Ashlan for the rest of the school year, first with her aunt, now by herself. She's 18, so I guess it's all legal, but she just seems so young to be acting so grown up. I haven't been to her place that much, but it is coming together nicely.

Erica's apartment is about what you'd expect a witch's apartment to look like. It is dark, small, and filled with witchcraft props of every imaginable type.

She has an entire bookshelf covered with jars and bottles containing herbs, essences, salts, and oils. Next to her bed, she has an altar to The Goddess. Under the Persian rug in the middle of the room, painted straight on the hardwood floors, is a pentagram that she uses as her circle for rituals and spells. She even has an old straw broom to sweep the circle.

"Even though I practice with the coven," she would tell you, "I really love the lone work, too."

We move the bookshelf into place and she quickly empties a few boxes of books onto it.

"I didn't have room for the essences *and* the books. But I really missed them."

I take a look at her books and notice a couple about dreaming. One is by Carlos Castaneda, and the other is by Oliver Fox. "Do you do much work in dreaming?" I ask her.

"Jeez, I wish. I have very little success with dreaming. I'm good at getting to the lucid state, but things tend to deteriorate pretty quickly right after that."

"That's pretty common," I say. "You should read your books more. You're probably using a lot of energy keeping your dreaming attention. It's not like walking around, where our perception is reinforced by the people in the world around us. You have to keep the dream world centered all by yourself. And you have to be sure your vibrations are just right to stay there a long time."

"How do you do it?"

"I use music to kind of change my vibrations, you

know? I descend on an instrument and resonate the proper note. My mom showed me that one."

"Well, I'm musically stupid, so that probably won't work for me."

"I can work with you," I hear myself saying. "Dreaming is sort of my strong point. I mean, my dad taught that meditation stuff for years, too, so it kind of has to be, right?"

"Potions are mine," Erica says.

"I know," I say, looking at the shelf of materials. "How about stones or crystals?" I ask, not noticing any.

"I keep a couple crystals around for protection, but I'm not as strong in it as I could be. How about you?"

"Um, I have a few stones, but not really any crystals. I don't know why, but I never got into them, you know? River rocks are great for dreaming, though. They help with projecting, when I don't have a lot of energy or I don't want to regress down."

Erica stops putting away books and looks at me wide-eyed. "You regress down?" she says. "Bullshit. And you just throw it into conversation like that?

All of a sudden, I'm a little hot and red, I can tell. I feel almost like I said something I shouldn't have. "Yeah, pretty often," I admit. Man, my ears are burning.

"What animals?" She's practically jumping up and down.

"Come on, this is embarrassing."

"No, don't let it be, Abbie, tell me." She's a child. An 18-year-old whiny child.

"Jeez, you know? It's not like you just go around talking about this stuff, Erica."

"Abbie, seriously, tell me about what you regress to. I'm so fucking interested I could die, okay? Just tell me."

"Okay," I laugh awkwardly. "I don't know, I'm usually some kind of big cat, mostly. Sometimes other things, though, like an owl, but mostly the cat." It's like I have butterflies in my stomach just talking about all of this to someone. Man.

"Wow. Can you show me?"

"It's easy, really," I say. "As long as you can get in the dream state and stay there, it's really easy. I mean, it's all a dream anyway, right?"

"Right." Erica turns her body to face me, sitting on her knees but with her spine perked up to attention. Those pale blue eye pierce right into me. "Do you practice scrying?"

"Yeah, I mean, a little, I guess. I'm not great." I notice that my body language is also one of interest and excitement. I never talk about this stuff, and it feels really good right now. It kind of makes me *more* nervous that it *does* feel so good; I feel almost guilty about it, but there's still a lot of excitement in sharing these thing with her.

"I've gotten pretty good," she says. "My mom uses a cauldron, but I have this totally different way that I learned from our priestess."

"What is it?"

"I use a couple mirrors and a vase. You'd like it, Abbie, you could totally use one of those vases you like so much. Let me show you, please?"

She rushes to clear a few bottles and candles off of the vanity next to her bed. "You have a mirror in your room, right? A big one?"

"Yeah, it's kind of like that."

"Okay, check this out. You set the vase with your water in it right here," she puts the vase about a foot in front of the mirror. "Then you put a candle behind it. I use a white candle because, well, you know, white candles for scrying, right?"

I nod.

"Then you sit here." She pulls a stool over to the middle of the room, and sits with her back facing the vanity. "And you look at the candle with this." She lifts a hand mirror and shows me how she looks at the vase over her shoulder in the reflection. "It's like, so cool, Abbie. I mean, you can just feel the energy in this circuit, you know?" She slumps a little, and smiles. Her hands are folded over her lap. "You know, we should really practice together."

"I don't know, Erica. It's not really my thing."

"Not regularly. Maybe just a ceremony or two. I can help you with some potions, you can help me with projection. Maybe we could even dream together and I could watch you regress."

"I don't know, Erica, jeez."

"I know!" Erica's eyes get wide. "We could do a Solstice ceremony together. Just to start out. It's a month away, and I like doing the Solstices without the coven."

I always tend to think of Erica in such a fake

light. Like she's always putting on an act, for some reason. I mean, her enthusiasm can be so damn annoying. But now, watching her sincerity and excitement, I can't help but see again what a beautiful person she is. She has an attractive light about her when she's spontaneous and happy. You just want to cuddle up in its warmth.

Looking at her right now, I think back to Samhain. I think back to the banishing list.

Seven

Teri was *resentment* on my list. I want so badly to find a way to replace my resentment with acceptance. I want to want to make her part of my life. My dad doesn't do things lightly, and having her move in with us was a big step in his life. If only I didn't have to resent the hell out of every fucking breath she takes.

I think these things as I stand at the sink, washing the vase that I bought. Teri is sitting at the kitchen table slurping coffee. And she is bugging the hell out of me. She takes these long obnoxious sips like she's in a Folgers commercial. She'll even smack her lips every so often and lets fly the occasional *ahhh*. It's disgusting when someone gets their behavior from what they see on a TV commercial.

I wash all my vases by hand once I get them into the house. Since I buy most of them second hand, I just hate to think of them coming into my house carrying baggage from their past owners. It's at least as much of a spiritual cleansing ritual as it is a physical one. I wash it with soap, geranium oil, frankincense powder, and a little rosemary.

I wipe the vase down with warm water, watching

the glass against my skin. Looking through the clear outer layer, I focus my attention on the emerald green inside. I reach my fingertips deep inside the jade glass, trying to make sure that I touch as much as I can of it. Again I notice that there's something about that green.

I snap out of my almost trans-like state and become suddenly aware of my surroundings. It's Teri's slurping that pulls me out of focus.

"That's a beautiful vase," Teri says. "A new requisition?"

Teri is, like, 30. That makes her 13 years older than me. That makes her 22 years younger than my dad. This means that my dad was 22 when she was born. Just graduated from college, and she was a newborn. She was a baby learning to talk, learning to crawl, learning to eat solid foods, and he was a man, learning to live in the real world, to pay bills, to take out a mortgage.

Dad didn't meet Mom until he went back to school for his Master's. Mom was an undergraduate music major. She was 10 years younger than him. Almost the difference between his daughter and his new girlfriend.

I just can't get over doing these little calculations all the time. Whenever I see them together, or whenever she talks to me, I do quick cross-references between math and social development to come up with reasons why they shouldn't be together.

When she was in sixth grade, giving oral history reports about ancient Roman life, he was becoming a father. When she was learning to drive, my dad was teaching lectures on Kierkegaard. When she was in college, my dad's wife was diagnosed with a previously unseen type of brain disease: irreversible. Two days after Teri graduated from college, my dad became a widower. I was orphaned of a mother. I was 12 then, giving oral history reports about Roman civilization. She was working as a receptionist at a psychiatrist's office. I was dragging my dad out of his bed and making sure he was taking his medications. When they met, I was the grown-up. I was missing school when my dad was on leave from the college.

Resentment.

I wanted to leave it behind in my Samhain ritual. I try to let it go. I try not to let her see the word in my eyes when she talks to me. She looks at my face and I worry that my eyes are spelling it, that she can sense it that strongly.

"Where did you get it?" she asks.

Pupils rolling up and around to form a letter *r*. Around and down in an *e*. "An estate sale." My pupils making a quick curve down to make an *s* in the middle of my blink.

"I think it's your prettiest one."

I try to remember how much better Dad has been since she came into his life. How he's been happy for almost two years. How he's actually started to wean off his medication. But my eyes roll again, make a loop and die, forming another *e* as I turn away from her and try to look back at the cabinet. "I don't know," I say. "There are plenty of others."

"Do you mind if we leave this one out? We could put flowers in it."

Oh God, she's walking over to me.

"Put it on the table. Or the mantle."

She reaches out to hold the vase in her own hands and I pull it away.

"Not this one, Teri. I think I want to keep this one in my room," I say.

"Well, what about these others?"

The letter *n* flashes in my eyes.

"Can we put some of these outs out? This house could use a more feminine touch."

I try not to mentally accuse her of thinking I'm a tomboy. "Umm," I say. "Yeah, a couple could go out. Let me pick them." I shuffle through the cabinet, reminding myself that she's trying to be nice. She's trying to reach out. She's trying to be friends. I should be thinking words like *acceptance, forgiveness, absolution, remit, melt, atone, amend, acquiesce.*

I pull out two plain looking ones. A crystal bud vase and a red disc vase. "Here," I say. "I just don't want the green ones out, you know?" I say. There are an awful lot of green ones, I notice.

"These are lovely," she says, knowing they're shit. "I'll find some flowers and put these out."

I don't want them filled. I want them empty. I want them receptive. I want them uninhibited. This is the resentment talking. This isn't me. This is what I was supposed to banish. I don't care what goes into the vases. I just care what she does with them.

"Thank you," I can hear myself murmur.

Eight

I play music at the Andante on Sunday nights. They charge a $2 cover on nights when they have live music. And I get half of that. Plus tips. It's never much, you know? On a good night, I might pull in $150, but I can generally count on maybe $75. It's my only source of income at the moment, and I try to make the money last me the week.

I quit my job at Starbucks when I thought it was interfering with my grades. I had a really bad semester and I just couldn't keep them up at all. But the next semester was worse. I got kicked out of my honors classes. Dad was so disappointed in me. I just hate to think of myself as the girl who ruined his little daughter. I just hate it.

I used to sing with some jazz group at a bar down the way, still near Mission Square. But it really wasn't my scene, you know? Just not the place for a 17 year old girl, even if she's as plain as me. The guys there kind of made me uncomfortable. It's like, I felt like some kind of beacon of youth, and they were always telling me how great I was and how far I can go at my age. I just didn't want to see myself like that, I guess.

Now I play solo, just me and my nylon string

guitar, and sometimes my cello. I play a few cover tunes - Iron and Wine, Dylan, Joni Mitchell, Deathcab - but a lot of originals, too. Nothing exciting, nothing too fast, or sexy, really. Just mellow and atmospheric. Passionate at times, I guess, but not sexy. I play for an hour and a half, and I also sell my self-produced CD.

As I play *"Ladies of the Canyon,"* I see a sight that has become familiar to me. At the table in the back, Erica and Vic sit next to each other, talking and laughing. They met a couple of months ago here. I usually don't mix friends, but since they were both always here, it just seemed to make sense.

Most of the time, I wish they had never met. I can tell that Vic is totally into her, and I know that she's perceptive enough to know this too, but enjoys dragging things out. To be honest, I have no idea how she feels about him, but she plays ignorant, and that is very irritating to me. God, what isn't?

What really bothers me about the whole thing is how they never listen anymore. I used to be able to look to the audience and see them both racked with attention. Vic would be seated in the corner, not touching his coffee, watching, listening, tapping his foot. Erica used to sit right up front on the edge of her seat, mouthing words, elbows on knees, not even sipping from her green tea latte. It's not like I'm some kind of ego maniac, or anything, you know? It was just nice to know that I was connecting with them.

Now they talk, laugh, and get up for refills during the show. They walk outside for a smoke twice a night, and Erica doesn't even smoke. I play something new, something that I worked hard on, and they don't even notice.

Afterwards they invite me out for a drink at another shop down the way that stays open pretty late. Someone is playing there, a poet and a guitar player, or something. They say it will be fun. They're all smiles and giggles and I feel like they're just asking me out to be nice or something. So even if I did want to go, I would have a hard time not feeling like I was cramping their action, you know?

But I just want to go home. I don't want my instruments hanging out in the trunk of my Volvo all night. I don't want to sit around and listen to them try to include me in conversation that bothers the shit out of me anyway. I don't want to be around their happy selves as they drink each other in.

So I tell them no. I don't want to go. No.

"Suit yourself," Vic says. First it was like they wanted me there, now I'm the one who's missing out, you know? Total bullshit.

I'm packing up my car when Erica rushes over to "make sure I'm alright."

"I'm fine."

"Are you sure? I'm not into him, if that's what you're worried about." She reaches over and holds my hands in hers. She shifts around her head so that she can look me in the eyes. She's so sweet.

"I'm not worried."

"You're the center of the spokes, Abbie. We want you there."

"It's Sunday night, Erica. Everything is going to

be dead anyway." I try not to sound upset or angry or resentful or anything.

"I just want to make sure you're alright."

"Why the fuck do you suddenly give a shit?"

Erica backs away like I just swung at her. And I don't blame her. I was surprised to hear myself say that, too. Like some kind of nerve was hit that I didn't even know was there.

"Fine," she says. "Jesus. When did you get so defensive and possessive?"

Possessive? I think to myself. Defensive? Two words that should have been on the banishing list. But two weeks earlier, they never would have made it.

All I want to do is go home and crawl into bed. I want to crawl in and give myself to the bed. Let everything melt away into the bed. I just want to crawl into bed and dissipate like the smoke, like I do when I project.

****

It's early, yet. I skip dinner and sulk in bed for a while. I spread out and feel its warmth.

Dad, of course, isn't one to just sit by and let me skip dinner. Before I've hardly had a minute to sit in bed, I hear his meek knock on the door. "Abbie," he says. "You there?"

"Come in."

My dad cracks the door slowly at first, and then steps in leaving the door open just a little. He sits on the edge of the bed and pats my leg. "You okay, sweetie?"

I roll onto my back and gather the blanket under

my chin. I don't like Dad to see what I wear to bed; it's a little skimpy and I don't want to somehow look slutty in front of my dad, you know? I feel like I should be wearing some kind of flannel old man pajamas or something. "I'm fine, Dad." I say.

Somehow, he's not convinced. "What's bothering you?"

And it's like the best question I've ever heard in my whole life. What is bothering me? I just can't really put my finger on it.

"Dad," I say at last, "why did you stop?"

"Stop what, sweetie?"

"You know, Dad, stop *practicing*?"

He takes a deep breath and lets it out in kind of a sigh. He turns his body to face me a little bit better. "Honey, I never really stopped."

"Yes you did, Dad."

"No, honey, I didn't really ever stop practicing, not like you think."

I sit up with my back against the headboard, still with the blanket up to my neck. "You did, stop, Dad. Don't act like you didn't stop practicing. Don't act like you're still in the Craft."

"Honey, I still meditate. I still have a mindful attitude towards life."

"But this isn't Buddhism, or whatever, Dad. Can you imagine how alone I feel in it sometimes?"

"Sweetie," Dad says. He's lit by the stripe of light coming in through the door and in this illumination he looks remarkably sad to be talking to me about this. "First of all, the Craft is different for everyone. So you can't really tell me if it's Buddhism or anything else. Magic is in everything we do. And besides, honey, there are other complications to my relationship."

"Your relationship with Teri? Should we really be letting our personal relationships get in the way with our religion, Dad?" I feel like I'm holding back tears.

"Abigail," he says coolly. "I was referring to my relationship with your mother, if you want to know. My relationship with the Craft is built around my relationship with your mother, and since she is gone, there is a hole that cannot be filled." Now I'm afraid that he is the one holding back tears. "So don't be so quick to feel like you're the only one alone here. I love you. And I love Teri. But your mother took more than just her heart with her to the next life. And Wicca just reminds me of her so much. This is just like school, Abbie; don't presume to know everything."

It's not like he was trying to hurt my feelings, but I thought he'd be a little more delicate with me. I slump back down into my bed with my head on the pillow. "Sorry, Dad," I say and turn my body to face the other way.

"I didn't mean to sound harsh, Abbie," he says. "You know how important you are to me. You know that I don't want to see you wrapped up in whatever kind of angst you're wrapped up in."

"Don't try and do that to me, Dad," I snap. "I'm not some angsty teen girl. I'm not having some kind of high school identity crisis here, Dad."

Dad surprises me when he smiles. "Honey, I said the same things when I was an angsty teen boy struggling with an identity crisis. These things are natural. They're a rite of passage. I just want you to know that no matter what is happening, with me, with Teri, or with your religion, I'm here. I'll always be here."

And yet, he stands up to go out the door. To go downstairs and talk the rest of the night to Teri. He feels like he's done his Dad job for the day; he gets to clock-out.

"Good night, Abbie," he says. "Get some rest and I'm sure you'll feel a little better about things."

Again with the trivializing. Acting like it's not a problem isn't the same as solving a problem. And just because I don't know what the problem is doesn't mean that it's not there. I think these things as he walks down the stairs.

Nine

I half-wake in bed, hearing whispers. I don't know what they are saying, but I can swear that I hear whispering in my ear. I'm not startled by this, though I feel like I should be; I'm just curious as to why I would feel like I'm hearing whispers.

I sit up suddenly and the whispers have gone away. It's maybe three in the morning, and I feel kind of restless. Although I'm hungry, I don't want to go downstairs to make anything. I don't want to wake Dad and Teri up. But I know that I can't just go back to sleep, since my head is so full of thoughts.

I'm thinking about the whispers. I'm thinking about Vic and Erica. I've never considered myself someone who gets jealous or needs a lot of attention. In fact, until I dyed my hair, I have always tried to be as invisible as possible when it comes to other people. But now, all of a sudden, I feel like I should be some kind of object of attention for Vic and for Erica, and like they shouldn't waste all their interest on each other.

I decide to do some scrying.

Scrying is a form of divination; a way to tell the future. There are plenty of different kinds of ways that people use to try and find out what is going to happen in the future. Many witches scry with a crystal ball. Others use a cauldron. But Mom used to say that you don't really need anything. That those are just props to help you give yourself visions. She told me that there are plenty of psychics, too. People who claim to see the future without ritual or magic. I've never met one, and I really can't imagine what that would be like; it seems almost burdensome.

I decide to try out the way that Erica taught me.

I prepare my room for the ritual and draw my circle. I sit in an uncomfortable straight-back chair in the middle of my circle, which faces away from the mirror over my vanity. In front of the mirror, I set a clear tear-drop crystal vase. In between the vase and the mirror, I place a tall white candle. I fill the vase with full moon water that somehow tints the vase yellow and blue. I light the candle and two cones of incense.

I sit in the chair and close my eyes. I try and clear my mind, concentrating on my breathing; breathing in the incense and letting it fill my body and mind. I try to feel my vibrations, like I do when I have an instrument, and try to lower them without the aid of the descending note. I imagine hearing the note played on my cello, lower and lower, darker and dimmer. I imagine a candle burning down, down, down. I try to make my body reflect these images, these sounds, and the lofty smell of the incense. I want to feel light and nimble, to feel my body float above the uncomfortable rigidity of the chair.

I use some of the things that Dad taught me about meditation. It's hard to concentrate and not be distracted by noises, even this late at night. But noises, I tell myself, only bring me deeper. Itches only focus my concentration more.

I open my eyes, my body resonating lower, my straight back feeling comfortable and relaxed. I can tell it hasn't taken too long, because the incense is still heavy in the air, and the candle light still flickers intensely on the walls.

I hold in my hand a mirror that belonged to my grandmother. It is old and heavy, framed in scrolled silver. The glass is foggy and scratched after years of use. I lift the mirror and look over my shoulder to the vase sitting on the vanity.

The water in the vase glistens with the light from the candle, amplified by the mirror behind it. The flame dances and changes, creating waves of light and shadows in the vase. Shapes fluid and smoky appear in the vase. I see something concrete growing in the shapes and waves of light and shadow. The light prisms in the ripples, creating a blinding rainbow at first, then it finally shifts and settles on a solid green.

Green like emeralds.

Green like leaves.

Green like the vase I bought at the estate sale.

Then the green moves in the water, pulled by its own gravity into a shape. I'm amazed, for an instant, at how well this session is going. I've never had visions this solid and I wonder if there is some special magic in

Erica's method. But I have to try not to think about it because I don't want to be distracted from what I am seeing.

After a minute or so of watching this splash of color move and shift, it forms an unmistakable image. A pair of stoic, unblinking eyes are staring back at me.

They are not staring just in my direction. They are not staring into space. They are looking at me, making eye contact. They do not examine a point in the distant future. They examine me.

They look deep into me and I feel vulnerable. I don't feel scorned, like when I get in trouble at school, but it's not far off. I feel more like I'm on display, a slave naked under the gaze of her master for the first time. I feel possessed, owned by the possessor behind these eyes.

My mother's words come back to me, words she spoke to me when I was just a child: "If something is happening to you that you don't welcome when you are in a trance, you have the power to make it stop. You can and should get out of the situation. You can turn it off. You are in control."

And yet I don't feel like I'm in control. I feel like I'm being controlled dramatically. I try with everything I have to resist this gaze.

And there is a shift. Suddenly there is a richness to the eyes. A seductive quality. A welcoming. I can feel it in the pit of my stomach, the same way I feel when I think of Vic's body being pressed on top of mine.

The beauty of the eyes becomes heartbreaking. It

feels like there is a weight on my chest that is pressing down. I can feel tears running down my cheeks and can hear smothered sobs in my throat.

The eyes blink for the first time. It's a long blink, and for the instant that they are closed, I feel free of this power over me. But when they open, they are not what they were. They are a deep, dark brown, like my eyes.

Everything ends quickly, like that dream you have of falling down right after falling asleep. The candle is just a candle again. The vase is just a vase. The water is just reflecting the light of a flame through it. No eyes. No fear. No weight. I am only a girl sitting in an uncomfortable chair in the middle of her room.

Relief, confusion, and excitement all vie for the prime emotion that I am feeling. They mix and marble together as I try to figure out what it was the scrying was trying to tell me. I have no clue as to what it means, but I've never had an experience while scrying that was nearly that intense.

Unable to sleep, I slip out of my window and hunker against the wall of the house wrapped in my heavy blanket, looking at the moon through the branches of the oak tree. The waning moon drops light through the branches, and I can feel the light replenish my spent energy.

Was it a sign? Was it a warning? Was it a beckoning? I just can't tell. Maybe, I think, it was an encounter. The thought frightens me and I want to be in bed, asleep.

I open a jar and pull out a small valerian root. I

chew it for a few minutes, then wash my mouth out in the bathroom. I fall asleep deep in the arms of my bed.

Ten

I wake up early to the sound of Erica's voice downstairs. She's talking to Teri, who doesn't work anymore, and asking to come up and see me. I'm way too tired for visitors, and I'm just wishing that Teri would send her away when I hear her say, "Sure, it's time she got up." Shit.

Erica makes a perfunctory knock on the door before trying to open it. She finds it locked, and I hear her humming to herself outside. I stay quiet, pretending not to hear her. Then I hear the lock being unlocked, and Erica steps into my room.

"Hairpin. These old locks can't resist them." She sits down on the bed, where Dad sat last night. "Wow, this bed is so freaking cool."

"Thanks," I say, turning away from her.

"I brought you some coffee and a bagel with strawberry cream cheese. Hurry up or we'll be late. You don't want to be late again."

"Cool. Put it on the vanity. But pour out the coffee in the bathroom if it's the same shit you brought me the other morning. And I don't care about being late. I think I just won't go to school today."

"Come on, Abbie," she shakes my body under the blanket vigorously. "I'm trying to cheer you up from last night." She's quiet for a minute. "Ooh, did you try my scrying method?" I remember that I didn't put things away after my ritual last night. It's so embarrassing that she should tell me about her ritual and then have it look like I rushed home to try it out. I really should have put it away. Even if I do plan to lock the door, I should have put it away.

"Yeah."

"How was it?"

"Just wait till I tell you," I say. I sit up and try and push my tangled black hair out of my face. Erica thrusts the coffee into my hand and I take a sip. It's much better than the day before. "It was the weirdest thing in the world."

"Wow, Abbie, that's beautiful."

"What?"

"Your eyes."

I take another sip of coffee. It's early, and I can't tell if Erica is coming on to me or what. Why is she complimenting my eyes?

"When did you get those? And should you really sleep in them?"

I look at my tank top draped loosely about me. She must think I look pretty sexy in it to be getting this kind of strange remark.

"The contacts," she says.

I stand up quickly and walk to the vanity. I push the vase and the candle aside and stare at my face in the mirror. Behind my messy black hair, are my two *green* eyes. The same eyes that I saw the night before in the vase. But instead of possessiveness and aggression, I see me; confusion, surprise, bags.

"Erica," I say very quietly. "Something very strange is happening to me."

"You're telling me. First the hair, now the eyes. You're turning into a new person. Soon you'll have different race. Or you'll be a dude or something. What's with all the changes?"

"Erica," I say again, very quietly. "I don't know what this means." I turn to her and see her through my new eyes. The world looks the same through them, but I am aware of their emerald newness. "Give me that bagel. Then we'll talk."

Eleven

Erica tries to convince me to talk to the elders of her coven. She thinks it's possible that they might know something about this situation that is just beyond my grasp. But for some reason, I don't want to bring anyone else into this. I want to buy sunglasses, or brown contacts, and hide from the whole thing. And yet, at the same time, I enjoy looking at people with my green eyes and imagining the image that they see: dark black hair, shining green eyes. It erases some of the plainness.

Erica has the closing shift at her Starbucks. After school, until she goes to work, we spend the afternoon together. We go to coffee. We go to her apartment. And the entire time, she can't stop staring at my eyes.

"It's really amazing, Abbie," she says outside the Andante. "Maybe you cast a spell without knowing it. Maybe there was something in the tea, or the incense, or something that you didn't plan on. It just doesn't make sense."

"It doesn't make sense, that's for sure," I say back. "But I didn't cast a spell. I'm sure of that, too."

I get up to go to the restroom and spend a long

time looking at myself in the mirror. I am becoming someone else, I think. The hair and the eyes make me almost unrecognizable. I wonder if I'm going to have to change information on my driver's license. The thought makes me laugh.

When I get back to the table, Erica bombards me with another suggestion. "I really think we should go see the High Priestess. These older witches are so much more experienced that we are. They've got to know something about something like this. It can't have never happened to *anyone* before."

"Erica, I don't want to have to keep turning you down. It's a fine idea to ask them about this. But I don't want to. I don't want to involve anyone, and actually, I'm starting to really like it. Maybe it's just a gift. A chance to change the way I go about things and become a more accomplished person."

"Green eyed people don't accomplish any more than their brown eyed counter parts."

"I mean, it's changing the way I see things."

"You know, you could mean that literally. If something has the power to change out your peepers, they can surely blind you. You could have something very dangerous and powerful on your hands. You might need to explore your room for something that has the power to do this."

"Jesus, Erica, you're so paranoid. My eye color changed. I wasn't fried up and fed to wolves, right?"

"But those feelings you had? They mean something. They at least mean that you have to be very aware of what's going on with you."

I think back to witchcraft trials; I'm glad I'm not party to one now. Changing eye color, I think, would be a dead giveaway that you're a witch back in settler times. I wonder how permanent this change is going to be. I wonder how many people I'll have to tell, "beats me, I just woke up one day and they were green. Nothing too strange about that, is there?" No, I'm glad that not many people know I'm a witch. If I am going to embrace this eye change, I'm going to have to at least come up with an excuse, or a motive, or something.

"Erica," I ask. "Why does someone change their eye color?"

"When they don't like how they look," she replies, and she's somewhat disgusted, I can tell. "It's called *vanity*, Abbie."

"Look into my eyes, Erica," I say. "Look into them and tell me, openly and honestly, are these honestly *my* eyes that you see?"

Erica sighs and puts down her coffee cup. She leans forward, looking into my eyes. She stares and blinks, and moves her head around. She reaches out and grabs my cheeks to shift my head, letting the eyes catch different angles of light.

"Abbie," Erica says. "The shape is the same, as far as I can tell."

"But what about what's *behind* the eyes?"

"You tell me, Abbie." She lets go of my face and leans back in her chair, and only now do I realize how close she was to my face. "I've been worried about you for a while now. And now this isn't even worrying you anymore."

"I can take care of myself, Erica. I don't need your damn church to watch after me."

"I'm not talking about that. I'm talking about what's happening to you in your life. The thing with Vic happened, for God knows what stupid reason. You distance yourself from him and from me. You change your hair color. You have absolutely no ambition to do anything with yourself lately. And now there's this. I just wonder if it's all coming from the same thing."

"Erica," I say calmly. "I'm fine. There's nothing wrong with me. I'm fine. My thing with Vic was stupid. I'm sorry if I've been moody. People color their hair all the time. And I didn't change my eye color—at least not on purpose. So stop worrying, and start being my friend."

"I'm always your friend."

We sit in the quiet for a while.

"Maybe," she says quietly. "Maybe you didn't cast a spell. Maybe someone cast a spell on *you*."

The thought seems obvious. Why haven't we come up with it before? But who would have cast any kind of spell on me, much less one that seems, at worst, docile.

"Don't forget how you felt. How you felt out of control. How you felt owned. Those feelings aren't random. Think of what happens when you don't consider the feelings in scrying."

I wake up in bed, hearing the whispers again. It's like the whispering is coming from all around me. I finally discern a phrase: "You don't need her." I open my eyes, but don't move. "She's not good for you." This time it is very clear, no longer a whisper at all.

"Who?" I ask quietly. There is a pause.

"The witch." Another pause. "Erica." This last part, her name, is almost spat out by the voice.

I sit up and look around. I see the moon light coming in through my window. I'm tired. I go back to sleep.

Twelve

I feel like I'm trying not to think about it all day Thursday. I stay inside and read most of the day. I love to read historical fiction, and I picked up a couple books at the library a few days ago. It's a wonderful escape for me when I read a story that is set in a realistic past. I know the events didn't happen, but I sort of think of them as occurrences in a parallel time frame of sorts. I take comfort in it somehow, the thought that we are connected to the past in more concrete ways than we realize. We often think of ourselves as so removed from our ancestors, from so-called lost civilizations, but we're built right on top of them. We are, in essence, an extension of them. And these novels make it all relatable, like they provide a wormhole to the past.

If only history class were so interesting.

What I'm not trying to think about is that I've made up my mind to go to Vic's show tonight. He hasn't called me or anything for a while now, but I'm still going to go. I need to know if I'm on the list or not. I need to know if he plans on still having an active friendship. Our friendship lately has felt like an empty house: it's still standing, but there's no life to it, no personality.

I read out on my balcony. I read in the study downstairs. I read in the bath. My bathtub is old and made of slippery porcelain. The control knobs are separate for hot and cold, but when you turn it on, you can feel the different water temperatures marble together. They're not mixed into an average temperature, but are forced into coexistence at the last possible minute before coming out of the faucet. For this reason, I stir the water for a while before climbing into the tub, with my foot. I stand there naked, hunched over the bath with just my foot wet in the tub, and I catch a glance of myself in the mirror.

I stand up straight and take my foot back from the tub. I study myself in the mirror for what must be the hundredth time this week. I look at my face, my hair, my eyes, and then I step back. I wonder what Vic must have thought of my naked body. I know he's seen other girls naked—I don't know how many girls he's been with. Just 17 and he's been around, if you believe what people say. He burns his life so brightly. I wonder if he turned me down because of my body, my skin. *Did* he turn me down?

He must find Erica more attractive. She's older, more mature, filled-out. Erica's eyes are so inviting, and her face has that comfortable roundness. She carries them with such confidence. She's so graceful and beautiful, it's no wonder he likes her more than he likes me. I'd choose her too, I think.

I lie down in the bath and hold my book, careful

not to get it wet. I try to soak the imperfections out of my body. Immersing my mind in the book, I try to soak rejection out of it too.

I take a long time to get dressed. I stand in front of the mirror in my room and try and paint different outfits on myself. I used to not care what I wore around him, and honest to god, I shouldn't care now. It's just that I feel somehow invited to come and see him play tonight. I finally settle on something casual enough, and try to slip past Dad and Teri without seeming like I'm preoccupied.

Vic's band is called The Discounted. Clever, right? Like they're on sale or like they are being passed over. He thinks it's pretty clever. Their music is characterized by a rich wash of sound, full of electric textures. Vic's voice is full, and probably leans towards the alto side of the spectrum. The words sort moan with emotion over the layers of sounds beneath them. They never play a single cover tune, and they'll play almost identical sets for weeks and weeks at a time; it takes them forever to practice through a new song. They play every Thursday at Stones, a bar near Mission Square.

Somewhat surprisingly, my name actually is on the coveted list, and I get in without paying the outrageous seven dollar cover charge. I never have asked him what he makes on a Thursday, but I'm sure it's at least twice what I make, even with his 5 person band. I look around for an empty table and can't find one. Then I see Derek, Vic's little brother sitting at a table by himself.

"Mind if I pull up a chair?"

"Hey, Abigail," he says. "You cost me seven dollars. Buy me a Pepsi?"

"No problem," I say, taking my seat.

Derek is a freshman. He skipped a grade somewhere in there, though you'd never know he was any kind of student. I've always guessed he was just some kind of prodigy. He's a nice kid, very nice, and never seems to be distracted. I've always been a bit protective of him, even if Vic hasn't been.

I wave down a waitress and order a Pepsi for Derek and a diet Coke for me. The band is taking the stage. The room is dark, with the occasional red lighting. The place looks like it should smell like smoke, but Ashlan's smoking ban makes the room entirely breathable. The bar is in the back, on the opposite wall from where the band plays. I see a figure approaching us in the dark. As she comes closer, I see that it's Erica. She carrying two bottles of what I presume is beer. As she sits down, I can see that they're Rolling Rocks.

"Hey, Abbie," she says, pulling a chair over from another table. She plops the beers down on the table before she sits down. "Okay, there are three of us. How are we going to split this up? Or should I go score another one?"

It's a relief to me to hear Derek say that he doesn't want one before I accuse Erica of corrupting the poor kid. I notice that Erica has a blue wristband showing the wait staff that she has been carded and passed. I don't ask her how, since I figure it has something to do with the way her boobs are bulging out of her dress.

"I'll have it," I say. I'm not a fan of beer. I like wine, but that's really about it for me. I honestly just don't want to see Erica sitting there with two beers to herself. It seems very sleazy to me for some reason, so I take the damn thing.

I haven't seen Erica since the night that I heard the voice in bed talking about her. I soften to her now as I sit next to her. Looking at the smile on her face, I am reminded of how kind and positive she is. There was just something about hearing that voice that had me dreading seeing her for the last couple of days. There was something convincing in what the words said. I thought for a moment about telling her about the experience, but I decided that it would be uncomfortable no matter what.

I notice and Erica and Derek have met each other, probably here, a few weeks ago. They talk like new friends together as we sit there waiting for the show. Derek is a shy boy and I have a hard time telling if he's flirting with Erica or not. Erica is just so open and, well, loud, that it seems like she's flirting with him. I guess maybe she just does that with everyone. And when I note this, my feelings are kind of hurt; I can't tell why.

The music starts and it becomes too loud to talk effectively. This is such a different venue from playing at the Andante. People here shout at each other, wander, mingle, and do a little listening as they, for the most part, spend their time drinking, buying drinks, and walking outside for a smoke. At the Andante, I feel like I provide a pleasant background that is worth giving your attention to on an unassuming night out.

The Discounted play for about 45 minutes or so. Their set is just about the same as it was last time I heard it, six weeks ago, right before sleeping with Vic. There's one added song, a slow one, the words are something about a burning Polaroid or some such emo stuff. It's pretty, restrained, and I imagine it as an acoustic piece; it would be beautiful.

The band packs up their equipment and the lights rise just a little before Vic comes and sits with us. On some nights there is a second band that takes the stage, but tonight that is the end of the entertainment.

"What did you think," Vic asks, sitting down. He's addressing us all, but looking at Erica when he says this.

"It was good," Erica says. "Nothing new this week?"

"You know, we just couldn't get it together. Rob didn't make a single practice this week, and we just couldn't do it without a drummer."

"Do what?" I ask.

"The new song I was working on."

"You played one that was new to me," I say.

"Yeah, it's a couple weeks old now. It's working much better now."

Derek stays quiet, mostly, no doubt admiring the way his brother has two girls hanging off his words. Soon enough, though, Derek points out that he does have school in the morning, even if the rest of us don't, and says he should really go.

"No problem, bro," Vic says. "Let me pay for my tab and we'll get out of here."

"It's on me," Erica says. "I'll take care of it tonight."

Vic grabs his guitar and he and his brother leave. The bar is still dark, but I can't help but feeling a little bit hurt that neither brother mentioned my eye color. It's not often you see such a drastic change in a person's looks, and they didn't notice. Now Erica and I are sitting on the table alone, she on her second beer, me barely nursing the second half of mine.

"So," Erica says. "Next month is the Solstice. What do you think about having a small ceremony, just you and me?"

"What did you have in mind?"

"Nothing big. You and me, outside up in the hills. It's a good time to meditate, to think about what has happened over the year. We can spend the longest night together up there, celebrating."

"Camp?"

"Why not? I have a great tent."

"It's freezing cold in the mountains this time of year."

"We can build a fire. We can bundle up. It'll be invigorating to spend the Solstice outdoors. On a brisk clear night in the mountains, there's nothing like the stars up there."

"As long as it's not snowing."

"Okay, as long as it's not snowing, let's do it. Maybe you can teach me a little about dreaming while we're there."

I usually spend the Solstice alone, like I do any holiday these days. But it sounds appealing to spend it with another witch, even if her customs are a little different from mine. I agree to it, though I'm not in the habit of making plans a month early, or at all really, right now.

We leave Stones at about midnight, and I am relieved to have spent the time with Erica, talking. The doubts about her that I've had since hearing that voice are gone. I write it off as just a normal, non-extraordinary dream. Those happen, I tell myself. When you have astral dreams and psychic dreams, your ordinary dreams can become more vivid and real. It's perfectly normal, and I try not to let something like a dream get in the way of my friendship.

THE TRAVELER

Thirteen

The night of December 13th, things change drastically for me. I go out to dinner with Dad and Teri, and we start talking about plans for the future. They are going out of town for the holidays, and they don't invite me. I'm not sure if they expressly didn't invite me, or they just didn't mention it to see if I would assume the invitation stood. In either case, I get the impression that there was at least an invitation to invite myself buried somewhere in there, but I don't take advantage of it because, honestly, I don't have a lot of interest in going to Old Mexico and taking an anthropological tour as a great way to spend the holidays.

What bothers me, whether I was invited or not, is that these plans were made completely separate from any sort of consideration for me whatsoever. My dad and I have always been really close, and we always used to make plans like this together. But now the plans just kind of popped up, with specific numbered dates and everything. They just sort of sprang it on me.

After talking about the villages and ruins that were on the agenda, Dad asks me if I was planning on acting like a good student next semester so I could go to college.

"I just don't know, Dad," I say. "I've been thinking that I would at some point. But if I'm going to major in music, I need to polish up quite a bit on theory and everything else."

"You could knock a few general ed classes out of the way, if you wanted to, sweetheart, before worrying about all that," Dad says. "I just hate to see you thinking about not keeping on with your education."

"Our concern is that you don't have any real pursuits, honey," Teri chimes in.

I bite my tongue. I try to think the word *acceptance* over and over in my head. Why the hell should Teri have any kind of concern about me at all, I wonder?

"I have plenty going on in my life," I assure them. "I am not unfocussed. At least not as unfocussed as I seem to be." But I can't really think of ways to back this up. It occurs to me that I don't ever think about school, and I don't miss work. I don't feel like I have time off, per say, but that the emptiness of my days are normal for me. I sound like a spoiled child who doesn't want to do anything with herself.

No conclusions are reached about my education, or my career, or anything else. But I do realize for the first time that I must be some kind of disappointment to Dad. He's so educated, so career oriented, and here I am not doing a single thing in the world, and might even throw away my chances to go to college if I don't pull my grades up soon.

When we get home, I head up stairs a little bit upset, despite the pleasant nature of the conversation. Dad and Teri go to the living room and open a bottle of wine; their Friday night ritual of reading and talking. I honestly wonder if this really "does it" for Teri. I know it's right up my dad's alley.

I get up to my room, and I decide to do a tarot spread. I'm tired and kind of depressed, so I don't want to go all out with a Celtic Cross format; I just do a simple three card spread, with the central question, *"What influences are surrounding my current path?"* This is a bit of a cheat. I usually don't like to ask such blanket statements. But with a three-card spread, you can gain access to a very generic situation.

I clear off my small nightstand and cover it with a silk scarf that I keep in my top drawer, wrapped around my tarot deck. I've never gotten fancy with my tarot cards; I still use the very basic deck, the Rider-Waite deck that Mom and Dad gave me when I turned 12. I shuffle them three times, concentrating on my question. Then, I place three cards face-up on the scarf in front of me.

The card in the first position represents my self, my ego, the root of why I ask the question. And, disturbingly, it is the Eight of Swords. This card shows a picture of a woman sitting up in bed and holding her face in her hands crying. Surrounding her in the air are eight swords, keeping her trapped and depressed. This card paints my current situation in a much more dismal light than I had realized it to be. It represents fear and anxiety; inconsolable unhappiness; and possibly an unfortunate event. I think that directly, it could be speaking about the emotional mess that I've been going through regarding Vic. And Teri. And the way that I don't want to face up to the reality of my life. I want to hide from it and watch it without trying to do anything to change it. *This is depressing,* I think to myself. I now realize just how childish I've been.

The second card represents the past influences—what brought me to this situation. It is card number 13. Death. A picture of a skeleton on horseback, carrying a black flag over people begging for temperance. This card isn't just about my mother dying. That's the most literal interpretation I get from it. This card also represents change. Change in myself. Change in my relationship with Vic. Change in my relationship with my dad. Change in the family structure in my home. This card is full of advice. This card tells me to learn from experience, not to fear change, that change is what we build our lives from. Yet all these changes have brought me to the eight of swords, so I'm not too happy about them.

At last there is the future situation, the immediate conclusion of present events. This card isn't supposed to represent my destiny, but the sudden outcomes of everything that I am doing in my life right now. And, like the two before it, this card is not good. Card number 16. The Tower. It has a picture of a castle tower being leveled by a lightning strike. It represents the fact that some changes are out of my control. Even worse, it's reversed.

The Tower reversed tells me that the process of

change has started and that no amount of clinging to the past is going to help anything. The Tower reversed gives me the advice to let go of everything, because my life as I know it will be turned into debris soon, and that something new will blossom in it's place. This would sound good if I had more positive cards in the other two positions. The Two of Cups and The World would have bolstered The Tower into telling me that on the other side of this, there is hope and peace and endless opportunity. But how it reads now, it just looks like I'm going from one despair to the next.

I thank the cards for being honest with me and for giving me a picture of what is in store for me. I pick up the three cards from the table, gently shuffle the deck one more time, then wrap it in the scarf and put it away. I meditate briefly about what they have told me. I dread the thought of going to sleep, of waking up, and of facing another day.

And it's that night that I see the first mark of The Tower.

I wake up in bed to hear the whispering again. I open my eyes. I'm lying on my side, and I can see my vanity across the room, the mirror reflecting the moonlight coming through the trees. I keep my breathing as slow as possible, hoping to distinguish words in the whispering. Tonight it sounds like chanting. I lie there and listen for what seems like half an hour, and the whispering definitely becomes chanting—chanting in a language that I don't recognize and cannot understand. The chanting slowly becomes song.

The singing is absolutely beautiful. I can't describe how the rhythmic and alien words permeate my whole body with a warm and calm understanding of comfort. The melody rises in what appears to be a pentatonic scale, sounding somewhat like an old Native American chant. But the rhythm is no longer as rigid and broken as a chant, but fluid and connected. I feel my body get lighter as I listen to the song's rising and crashing, up and down the pentatonic scale. I'm mesmerized and so at peace that I feel as relaxed as if I were sleeping.

After a long time, the singing stops. I know that a good amount of time has passed, because the light from the moon through the window is at a different angle than it was before. I lie there for a while longer, and finally decide that the singing isn't going to start up again.

I stand up to go to the bathroom. As I walk to my bedroom door, I hear a rustling coming from behind me. I turn around and feel like the air has been knocked out of me.

There is a figure lying in the shadows in my bed.

I take a deep breath to regain my composure, and I don't make a sound out of pure fear. I step closer, hoping to reveal this to be nothing but a trick of shadow and light; the kind of trick that used to keep me up nights when I was young until Dad would come and chase the monsters out from under my bed for me.

I get closer and I can see quite plainly that there is a girl lying in my bed, facing away from me. I'm not frightened, however, because I can see now that it is probably just my body. At some point I must have done something to leave it, and I am standing here on an astral plane looking at my physical self.

Just as I think this through fully in my head, my muscles loosen and a sigh comes out of my lungs. But again I am frightened to the point of falling when the girl sits up in bed, startled. I try to scream from the floor, but I am unable to, and she climbs to the edge of the bed and peeks over at me.

"Abbie, are you okay?" she says.

I don't say anything in return, but crawl backwards towards the door of my room.

"I was starting to think you would never wake up," she says. "Don't be scared. Don't you know who I am?"

The voice is soft and familiar, completely unthreatening. I struggle to find the door knob over my head. I turn it and try to force the door open.

"You *pull* on the knob, honey," the girl says. "Please don't be scared. You'll hurt my feelings."

There's sweetness in her voice that I can almost see. There's no doubt in my mind that this girl was the one singing only moments ago. I don't feel threatened by her so much as startled and unprepared. She's beautiful, but her face is wrinkled with concern. She's maybe a couple years older than I am, but with the same straight black hair. I cannot make out her face clearly because a shadow rests across her left side.

"Abbie," she says. "Just relax. Don't you remember me?"

I try to speak, but my voice cracks. I take a couple very deep breaths, then squeeze out, "Traveler?"

Her face softens. "Oh, Abbie. It's so good to see you again. I've missed you so much."

I pull my legs, splayed out in front of me, up to my chest and try to sit calmly against the door. I can feel my heart beating in my throat and my muscles ache with adrenalin. I take deep breath, mimicking my breathing exercises for meditation. Traveler sits quietly and patiently, watching me grow accustomed to her presence.

"Take your time," she says. "I never thought this would be so scary for you, or I wouldn't have sprung this on you like this. I feel so bad."

"Traveler," I say at last, almost in a whisper. "How can this be real? Is this real?" She nods, with a smile on her face. "How have you been?"

She laughs and does this quick little flutter kick with her feet in excitement.

"Oh, Abbie, I knew you would be okay with this," she says.

"Okay with what, Traveler?" I ask.

"Okay with me coming to see you."

I can feel that I am much more relaxed now. *The worst of it is over,* I tell myself. Now I'm just seeing things, or something. Now I'm just hallucinating. Now I'm just losing my mind.

Ok, I am dreaming, after all.

"I think I'm okay, Traveler. I mean, I'm just surprised, right? I didn't think...you know, that you were really, you know, real. Just don't scare me so much next time," I say. I lift myself up and walk hesitatingly towards the bed. And her.

I get really close, and she is sitting on the edge of the bed now, smiling.

"Your hair is beautiful, Abbie," she says. "If I do say so myself." She flips her hair playfully. "And don't get me started on those eyes."

"My eyes? What do you mean? Do you know anything about my eyes?

"You got the better deal, Abbie." Traveler leans forward and I see her entire face. She blinks her eyes and they are unmistakably brown. In fact, they are unmistakably *my* brown eyes—the same eyes that I had seen the green ones change to in my scrying vision.

I am startled by this, and suddenly find myself sitting up in bed, awake, with the morning light pouring through the window. I'm dizzy and my head aches like hell. I think that this must be what a hangover feels like, but I didn't have a thing to drink last night. I stumble to my feet, look back at my bed, and head off to the bath, taking two aspirin on the way.

Fourteen

I'm sitting outside the Andante, drinking a latte and pretending to read a book.

>But really I'm thinking.
>And thinking.
>And thinking.

Fifteen

There was a time when I was young that my parents were fighting. I don't remember what they were fighting about now. It doesn't matter. Every one of my parents' fights are scarred into my memory, but I don't remember one thing that they ever argued about particularly.

It was late at night, and I was in the second grade. I huddled in my bed, listening to the arguing coming from down stairs. All their arguments were always at night, and I think they thought I slept through them; they saved up their fight all day long and let them loose at night to try and save me from it. It just made it worse, in my mind. I hated being woken up by the sound of argument.

I shut my eyes tight and sunk down into my bed, under the covers. Down there already was my imaginary sister, Traveler. Her bright green eyes nearly glowed in the darkness under the sheets.

"Hi Abbie," she said.

"Hi Traveler."

"What are they fighting about this time?" She sounded like she was near tears.

"I don't know."

"I hope it's not about us."

"They wouldn't fight about us, would they Traveler?"

"Abbie," Traveler said in a consoling tone. "It's really hard to raise kids. I bet that Mom and Dad are fighting because they are sad about missing their dreams. Mom wanted to play music and Dad wanted to see the world."

"Mom's not sad. She does play music," I said meekly.

"Abigail, Mom didn't just want to sing you lullabies and show you how she can play cello. She wanted to play in front of audiences. She wanted to play with the Vienna Symphony."

"What's that, Traveler? Is it a song? She can play it to me. We can tell her that she can play it to me."

"Oh, Abigail, it's not a song. It's only the best orchestra in the whole world in the most beautiful place in the whole world. You should see the mountains and forests of Österreich and Byern, Abigail, you would never come back to this silly little town."

"Where?"

"Don't worry about it, Abbie. You're too young to know things like this. It's just that Mom and Dad didn't imagine their lives being so tied down as they are now."

"But they *love* us, Traveler."

Traveler looked thoughtful and nodded. "They do now. But Dad misses the places he used to go before he was married. Dad misses seeing the Pyramids, and the Incan cities. Dad's been to the ruins on Machu Picchu. He's seen the Kamilari tomb on Crete. And Pompeii. Do you think he could really be happy spending all his time in Ashlan after seeing all the things that he's seen?"

I was crying by now. I wasn't sure what exactly she was saying, except that Dad wasn't happy being with us, and that Mom wanted more than just me.

"Don't cry, Abigail. You should be careful to not cause any more problems for them, okay? We both need to be careful."

"Okay."

"Remember that no matter what happens, you'll always have me."

"Okay."

"I mean it, Abbie. No matter what else happens in your life, you can count on me. You can listen to me. Do you understand, Abigail?" She was holding and hugging me, and I felt so very *needed*. "Now, lie back down and I'll sing you a lullaby."

I put my head back on my pillow and shut my eyes. I heard Traveler say, "This song is from my grimmerie." And she sang a long, slow, song in a high whisper. It wasn't altogether different from the song she sang to me the other night when I woke up in bed.

I haven't really thought about Traveler in years. I mean, I remembered that she was there, that she was my imaginary sister, but I never thought much of specifics. Just like how I never thought much about the games I played on the playground or the pictures that I drew on children's menus in restaurants. But now our conversations are coming back to me. They are coming back to me in a landslide of realization - specific words aren't muddled or missing, they are all there completely. It's like just talking to her the other night was a key that opened the door to all these memories. They are parallel memories, not mixed in with my other ones. Like they were from a different world, or a different life. I can't remember the context of most of my visits with her, but I can remember the conversations complete and separate from my normal life.

One thing is for sure, Traveler is more than I gave her credit for.

I remember now, how Traveler told me about things that I never could have imagined. She told me about places and people that I never could have known about. And she taught me spells. She taught me how to make incense and bath salts.

"You have to listen carefully, now, Abbie," she told me one night. "You're going to have to gather some ingredients from Mom's shelf. You can't write this down, so you have to remember very carefully."

I sat at attention, sensing the seriousness in her tone.

"I need you to get lotus oil. And a sprig of rosemary. Go to the pantry to find some sea salt. You'll need to make that incense I taught you about. Do you remember how to make it?"

"Sandalwood, makko, sage, and oil boiled from the cactus in the front yard," I said. "It'll be a couple days before it's ready, Traveler."

"That's okay. We have to wait for a new moon anyway. We have two weeks, but I want you to be very prepared. Mom has a dark and fragrant tea in the pantry next to the coffee. It's been there a long time, so check it for mold, but it should be fine. I'm going to tell you how to use an infuser, because it's very important that you not drink a single leaf of that tea."

Her instructions were always detailed and rigid. I followed them to the very last step, finding that I had an excellent memory for her instructions. In retrospect, I may have learned as much about the craft from her as I did from my mom.

And music, too. Traveler sang and played a wooden flute. My mom taught me string instruments, but it must have been Traveler who taught me to play that strange flute.

"Abbie," she said one night. "It's time you learned a little more about dreaming. It's time you learned how to become an animal."

"Why?" I'm not sure how old I was then. I think it was the last year I had the bed. Just before Grandma came to live with us.

"It can do wonderful things for your energy, in dreaming and in life. When you can become part of the landscape, you can gather new kinds of energy from the Earth and your powers will increase. Everything will work better for you.

"The first thing you have to do is get even lower in vibration than you are now. I've got an incense recipe for you. And a new tea recipe. You'll need to go out and buy a good wooden recorder or Native American flute. Just until you can carve your own."

And again I followed her directions to the very end.

And I can't say that I regret it.

Part II—Traveler

Sixteen

"How often do you dye your hair?" Vic asks.

"Just the once."

"How long ago was that? A month anyway, right? It hasn't faded one bit."

"It's black, Vic. Black on blonde hair isn't going to fade very much," I reply. "Especially with the way that I dyed it." We are sitting inside the Andante on a Sunday after I played a show. He came by himself and sat close to the front, near the stage. He listened the whole time. And now he's taking notice of my hair.

"But there are no roots."

I thought back in my head. When did I dye my hair? Right after Samhain, and now it was almost the Winter Solstice. Over a month and a half. I probably should have light roots coming in by now, but I don't.

"I cast a spell on it, right?" I joke.

"Cast the same spell on mine so I'll never go gray," Vic says. Then he sits there for a while, not smoking his cigarette, but looking at it. It's chilly out and the small glow at the end of the cigarette looks warm and inviting. "You were good tonight." He finally says.

I don't say anything in return. I know I was good, and there was a big crowd. Well, pretty big for me, anyway. I'm finishing counting my tips and I find that tips plus cover, I made about $170; probably my best night ever.

"You really raked it in, too," he says, seeing the smile on my face as I wrap a rubber band around all those ones and fives.

"It was a good night," I nod. "Where was Erica?"

"Beats me."

"She hasn't missed a show of mine in a while," I say.

"Do you want to go for a walk?" Vic asks.

"Why?"

"They have all the Christmas lights up the neighborhood. I thought it might be fun to walk down Meadow and see all those nice houses decorated."

It was all I could do to hide the huge smile that was trying to sneak out onto my face. It was working. Two nights before, Traveler walked me through a love spell. The spell, she told me, wasn't supposed to make him fall in love with me, exactly, "Because that's just silly," Traveler explained. "I've never heard of a love spell that can actually make someone fall in love."

"Then what does it do, Traveler?" I asked.

"It makes him see you without distraction, is really the best way I can put it," she said. "He'll look at you and *notice* you. Imagine taking a picture with a really nice camera, you'll be in focus and everything else will just kind of blur out when you're around."

"How?"

"We bind him to your essence. He'll see you with his filters off; no baggage, no distracting noise, just you. You're going to need something of his, and something of yours. For you, we should really use your blood. It would work better if we could use *his* blood, too, but I doubt you want to walk up and cut him." She had a smile that told me that she would enjoy the spectacle of me trying to get blood from my friend.

"Yeah, I don't think that's a good idea. But what else can we use?"

"Fluid is best, but we can work with hair. Do you think you can manage to get a pretty good size strand of his hair without being obvious or seeming desperate? I don't know, Abbie, maybe this one is a little beyond you."

"No, no Traveler, I can do it. I'll just tell him I need it for a spell."

Which is exactly what I did. He laughed me off, and then, after I insisted, he gave me a strand of his hair that had fallen onto his shirt. I took it, and nonchalantly put it in my pocket, making it look like I was being so haphazard and comical that I was surely kidding.

"Anything else that will be hard to get? I can do it," I said.

"You have most of what you need on your shelf. But this is a complicated spell. It has to be done half in your world and half in mine." She went over the details of it with me. What incense to burn. What tea to drink. What to mix in what quantities. And, finally, when to meditate into her world and complete the spell with a song and incantation that she would help me with. The spell took all night to do.

Spell work has never really been my thing. Dream work came naturally to me, or rather, I suppose, Traveler always helped me with the dream work. But casting a spell has always been such a complicated process to me. And I never really saw the reason to cast a spell of protection, or binding, or one of profit, or blessing, or overcoming an obstacle, or any of the other spells that are outlined in my family's grimmerie. I was always happy to stick with the part of the craft that didn't involve spell weaving.

Spells are complex. They're not just recipes; it's not like baking a cake. It's an appeal to forces beyond our understanding. You don't just mix ingredients and wait for things to take shape. You approach it with the proper attitude. You spend days beforehand gathering up the energy to do it, because you send that energy out in exchange for the spell working. Spells are full of literal magic and symbolic gestures, which put your awareness and intent to work to get a job to be done. To be done right, you have to live your life right. Your energy has to be balanced. In short, you have to deserve it.

At any rate, now the spell is working and Vic is pouring his attention on me.

"You sounded really good tonight," he says.

"I heard you the first time," I say.

"I didn't know that I said that already. I mean, really, really good. I was thinking about that one song about the river, did you write that?"

"No," I say. "Are you an idiot? That was Gordon Lightfoot. It's a wonderful song."

"No kidding."

To be honest, it's a little embarrassing listening to him like this. He's so full of sincerity and interest that I hardly know what to do with him. It's cold out, and the fog is starting to roll into the valley, so all the Christmas lights have these little halos of colored brightness around them. All I can see of Vic is his silhouette. He keeps brushing up against me, and I keep waiting to feel his hand reach for mine, but it doesn't.

"I was thinking that maybe we could play together sometime."

"Play what," I say. "Chutes and Ladders, or like, Doctor?"

Vic laughs, and the sound comes out of his mouth looking like smoke in the cold Christmas lights. "Music," he says. "You have a beautiful voice. And you're really not bad on that guitar. But it's that cello of yours that brings me to tears."

"That makes sense," I say. "There's just something about the cello, you know, it's the same size as a person. It's the perfect vibration to make you really *feel* the music."

He thinks about this for a minute, or is at least quiet. "Yeah," he says at last. "That makes sense to me. Those strings aren't much longer than a guitar's."

"No, but they're thicker. But it's really the wood," I say. "The strings vibrate against the wood, and the wood takes those vibrations and amplifies them, rings them out. The size of a cello is perfectly the size of a torso. When you play one, you can feel it ringing in your chest and in your gut. And it feels so good. You get lost and absorbed in the sound."

"I should play acoustic more often."

"We can play sometime, Vic. If you really want to."

"I think I'd like that," he says.

And now I feel his palm reach over and grab my hand. He holds my hand gently and without much fanfare; there's no rubbing or squeezing. Just my hand being suspended by his.

Vic has this song that he wrote a long time ago. I always thought it was about me. The line goes: *"All she ever wanted, all she ever needs, is for me to say I love her, and a drug to make it real."* And that line keeps playing over and over as we walk. The next line goes: *"It's a crime for me to sit here, pretend she's in my head, but my cold and twisted covert makes me say what she wants said."*

It could have been about me, I think. But it could have been about any of the girls he's been with.

I squeeze his hand, and I can see, even in the dark, that he's smiling.

Sol Smith

Seventeen

"It's going well," I tell Traveler. "I had a better night with him than I've had in ages. I mean, I really have to thank you."

"And," Traveler says. "Don't you feel less adrift? Don't you feel more rooted, more secure, knowing that he's falling for you?"

I think about this for a moment. "I'm not sure," I reply. "I feel good. I feel tickled and excited to get this kind of attention. And I'd be lying if I didn't say I was a little turned on by it." I look at Traveler, and her brown eyes are attentive and focused as I speak. "But I don't see how this is really *doing* something about my life," I continue. "I mean, having you with me again, can't we do just about anything? If we can get him to fall for me, you know, after he's already sort of decided against it? What stop here, Traveler?"

"Abigail," she says, "witchcraft is not about wish fulfillment. I won't have you going off and making ascertains about what you *think* you want. Remember that it was your little confused mind that got us into this situation."

"I guess."

"And it's my guidance that is going to get you back on track. You wouldn't believe how many people live their lives off track. If you want to become who you were meant to be, you will listen to what I have to say."

"You're right, Traveler, you're right."

"Your energy, your personal power was diminished when he had you and walked away. You only have do much *intention* and you just handed it out for free. That's means you're running a deficit and you have to get it back," she looks at me and nods, as if agreeing with herself. "You're wrapped up, you can't see it well. You have to bow down to someone who has the long view of the situation. You're simply too close to the whole thing to make your own decisions. But, I am glad that you're enjoying this new attention from Vic."

"I am, Traveler, I really am. I didn't at all mean to seem ungrateful. I'm very happy to be in control of our relationship again."

"That's good, Abigail. I'm proud of you. You're doing the right thing."

In the weeks since Traveler has been in my life, I've talked to her every night after going to sleep. She has guided me through this latest spell as if no time has elapsed between now and my tutelage as a child. And all along the way, she has promised to help me get out of the rut that I've found myself in. She's promised to help me find myself again, and she's said that the first step is getting Vic back into my life.

"The senseless use and rejection you experienced at his hands has really drained your aura," Traveler tells me again. "If you get him back, it'll replace all that spent energy. It'll affirm to the universe that being with him wasn't a mistake; that it was the first push that needed to gather momentum. Get him back, and establish your right to him, and then you can do whatever you want with the situation. Remember, witchcraft practiced by women isn't about the subservience and usefulness of our gender, it's about our power and esteem."

"It's not that I don't believe you, Traveler," I say. "It's just so forceful, you know?"

"Don't worry," she says. "Trust me on this. It will all come together perfectly. You're doing wonderfully."

"Thank you, Traveler. I've really love having you back. Will I see you tomorrow night?" I ask.

"Why wouldn't you?"

"I'll be up in the mountains with Erica. Can you visit me there, or do you kind of stay with the bed?"

Traveler seems a little hurt, and then embarrassed. "I didn't realize that was tomorrow. Now that you mention it, I'm kind of stuck with the bed. But let's not worry about that right now. There's time enough to worry about that later."

"Oh," I say and look at her. She doesn't return my look. "I've never really considered it, Traveler," I say with concern.

Her face goes from solemn to irritated. "We have much more pressing problems, you know. We need to make sure that you don't steer away from your immediate goals. Are we very clear on this point, Abigail?"

"I'm doing everything you tell me to, Traveler. Is there anything wrong?"

"Yes, there is."

"What is it, Traveler?"

"You shouldn't be hanging out with that amateur witch anyway," she says. "She's not here to help you."

"What do you mean? I love Erica."

"Abbie, please, listen to your sister," Traveler reaches out and puts both of her hands over mine and looks into my eyes. "Erica is holding you back. She's been holding you back since she brought you up to that hokey group of ninnies up in the hills. She's not looking after you. She's keeping track of you."

"What do you mean?"

"Abbie, can't you tell? Haven't you felt how she has been manipulating you? You've seen how she looks at him."

"At who?" I say, but I know the answer to this and Traveler glares at me like a disappointed mother.

"She wants him bad. And if she keeps you close, she knows that she can keep track of what you're doing with him."

"No, Traveler," I say. "She doesn't want Vic. You have to understand. She flirts with everyone. That's just how she is, you know?"

"That's what she wants you to believe," Traveler says. "And I really didn't want to have to tell you all of this so soon, honey."

"Tell me what?"

Traveler just closes her eyes and shakes her head.

"Please, Traveler. I can handle it. I'm not the little girl that you remember; I can handle all of this now that you're back. Don't worry about hurting me."

Traveler holds my hands again, and looks into my eyes. "Abigail, is there any doubt in your mind about how serious this all is?"

"No, Traveler, I understand. You've been very honest with me about it all."

"That's right, Abigail, I have been. But I've been keeping something a secret, too. Because you *are* that little girl that I remember, in so many ways. Because you have such an innocent view of life and you can't see the forest despite the trees so often."

"You don't have to be gentle with me, Traveler."

"Yes, Abbie, I do. Because you're not going to like what I have to say."

She's so serious now, and I'm afraid that she's right; I won't like what she has to say. "Traveler," I say at last. "I trust you. And if you don't want me to know, I can forget that this conversation even happened. I'm sorry if it looked like I didn't trust you. Of course you know what's right."

"Abigail, it's too late. The door is opened and we have to walk through it. It's unfortunate that it has to happen so soon, is all."

"I'm ready for what you have to say, Sister."

Traveler takes a deep breath. "Erica has a binding spell on you."

"What?"

"Why do you think you've been so lethargic? Why do you think you feel like you're wasting your life all of a sudden? She's holding you back. She's trying to make sure you don't threaten her."

"No, Traveler." I take my hands back from hers. "You don't understand. She's my *friend*."

"She's no friend of ours, Abbie." Traveler is near tears. "You can do whatever you want about tomorrow night. Spend your Solstice with whoever you want to. I won't be hurt. I won't even know that the time has passed when you get back. But I have to urge caution, Abigail. Whatever she does to you can be undone, but I still want you to be watchful. I still want you to remember which of us is the wiser. Watch her. Remember when she put something in your coffee?"

And now I feel like what she's saying might be true. Now I feel like something isn't quite right. I trust Traveler. I consider her my sister. And I never have fully trusted Erica, for reasons that I could never distil.

"Go up with her," Traveler says. "Keep *her* close. But don't trust her. Watch her. Be her friend. But have your guard up. Perhaps that will help us out of this situation with her."

"Traveler, this is coming as a shock to me. But I have to thank you."

"Please, Abigail, don't thank me. It pains me to ruin your innocent view of the world around you." Here, she holds my chin and points my face at her. "Don't thank me."

"But I have to. You've opened my eyes, Traveler. I'll be on my guard, okay?"

"I didn't want to have to address this yet," she says. She stands up and walks over to the window, looking out. The moonlight - nearly full - bathes her body. She is a beautiful woman. I remember as a girl, I thought that I imagined her this way so that she would embody everything I wanted to look like. She still does.

"It's a good thing I'm back in your life now," Traveler says, looking out onto the backyard. "Mom was right to have you bring the bed back into your room. She knows what she's doing, Abbie."

"Do you ever talk to Mom, Traveler?" I get up and walk over to her by the window.

"No, Abbie, I don't. I miss her so much." There's sadness in her voice that is heart wrenching and I can see that tears are welling up in her eyes. She shuts them tight and sniffs loudly. "I haven't seen Mom for far too long."

I watch her in the moonlight. She sits down on the cedar chest that rests under the window. She bows her head and I notice she has blonde roots growing in under her black hair. She has the roots that I don't have.

"We don't have a lot of time to waste," she says. "We don't spend a lot of time together on these nights. And there's so much to do that's relevant. I hate to waste time being sentimental."

"No, no, Traveler," I say. I sit down and put my arm around her. "It's okay. I miss her, too. And I'm so sorry that I spent so much time away from you. Do you get lonely?"

She smiles under her tears. "Like I said, Abbie, there's not a lot of time to waste on things like that. When we get you up on your feet and in control of your destiny, well, then we can spend all the time in the world being sisters at night in this room."

I hug Traveler and feel her arms wrap tightly around me. With my face buried in her neck, I can smell birch and sandalwood in her hair. I rub her back, feeling the silky cloth against her skin underneath. She sobs into my shoulder and I stay there, gently swaying my big sister, far into the second longest night of the year.

Eighteen

Erica is driving me up into the mountains. She picks me up in her truck and I throw my sleeping bag, a cooler full of food, and my duffle bag into the bed of her truck. She has the camper shell on the bed, "just in case it's too damn cold." I climb into the cab, and we drive off.

We drive through downtown to get to highway 180. From there, it's a straight shot to the Sierras. The cityscape gives way to neighborhoods - houses with yards and trees, churches with tall steeples and gaudy signs, high schools with stadiums, and grocery stores with acres of parking lots. The neighborhoods give way to farmland - fields of grazing cattle, row after row of peach trees, and grapevines stretching as far as the eye can see in immaculate stripes, turning into almond orchards, and oranges, and plums, and lemons. The farms fade away and we enter the foothills with their rolling expanses of dry fields with sparse scrub and trees, arching, ending, curving back, up and down, up and down. The foothills go up sharply to the mountains proper. As the altitude gets higher, so do the trees. From oaks and ash to evergreens and redwoods, the landscape goes from a spent dry golden-brown to towering greenery. Then there are patches of snow, giving way to fields of snow. There hasn't been a lot of snow up here at this time of the year, but several inches are expected next week.

Touching the window, I can tell the temperature outside has dropped at least 20 degrees from the valley floor. The half-circle knob on the dash - the one with a tiny sliver of heat-indicating red on one side and a thick block of it on the opposite side - has been slowly moved from left to right, from barely on to high.

We talk a lot about the ins and outs of our camping trip. I've only been camping a handful of times, and never in the winter. Her family, Erica tells me, always camps. We're actually going to land that her family bought up there with the plan of eventually moving, but for the time being, they just camp up there several times a year. She has a tent, she tells me, a good one. And just to be safe, she brought along plenty of wood for a big, warm fire. I'm still nervous, and pretty sure we'll find ourselves in the car before the night is out, engine running, heater on.

"So," Erica says to me, after a brief pause. "How did you learn so much about dreaming? In our coven, we only really touch on dreaming once in a while. We're much more in to ceremony, ritual, spell weaving, that kind of thing."

"It's always been a part of my teaching," I say. "My mom stressed it from the time I was little. My dad stressed the meditation and relaxation stuff that really leads to dreams. Dreams have always just been another side to my life, not something peripheral or alien. Not much on ceremony, I guess."

"I've been doing a lot of reading about dreaming lately."

"I saw the books we put up on your shelf. Did any of them help at all?"

"I don't know," she says. "Maybe a little, but nothing clicks for me, you know? When I do realize that I'm dreaming, I usually lose control pretty quickly."

"There's your first problem."

"Losing control?"

"No, that's your *second* problem. Your first problem is that you realize you're in a dream. You've got to get past that."

"Isn't that the first step?"

"Recognizing dreams can be really hard, I know. But you have to go beyond exploring the dream state by chance. You need to *invite* the dream state. You need to enter it on purpose. Stop playing defense, play offence, as my dad says."

"How do I do that?"

"Lots of ways," I explain. "Meditation. And guiding yourself down into the dream state. I can get to the dream state while lying down in my bed in less than a minute most of the time. If I'm trying to get really deeply into it, I have to sit up and use other vibrations to guide me down."

"There are different levels?"

"Well, yeah, you know? We're in one level right

now, right? I couldn't tell you exactly how many levels there are, but I don't know, probably infinity. As you get deeper and deeper, the rules of this world can bend more and more. You get closer and closer to the essence of things. You can borrow their perception, their energy, and their power."

"See," Erica says. "This is the stuff I'm reading about that I keep finding so hard to believe."

"The idea that there are all these worlds right here in front of us, if we could only see them?"

"Exactly. But tell me about using other vibrations."

"I learned a pretty neat method when I was younger to use an instrument and follow its descending vibrations lower and lower. It was tricky at first, but it works really good now. The lower you get, the more sophisticated the interaction between worlds can be."

"Wow," Erica says. "Listen to you and your words. Do you think you could show me sometime?"

"I don't really see myself as much of a teacher, you know? But I can sure try. You'll just have to be real patient and not try and expect anything, right?"

We end up being about five thousand feet up. Just high enough to feel the difference in the air density. Erica pulls off the highway onto a gravel road and gets out to open a metal gate. When she opens the door, I can feel the brisk air come in. I'm not ready for this; I'm afraid. The sun is still way up and it feels colder than I want it to.

We drive in for about half a mile before she stops in a clearing about a hundred feet across in a rough circle. Towards the edge of the clearing is a large stone circle that I assume serves as the fire pit. Ten yards away from the fire pit is a big shelter, a roof with no walls, like you see picnic tables under in the park.

Erica hops out of the car excitedly.

"This is where my family is going to move." She opens her arms out wide, thinking I will be very impressed. "We're going to have a compound."

"A compound?" I ask.

"My parents want to build here someday. My sister and her family are going to build over by those trees. I'm going to build in a clearing down the way when I have a family, if I want one. The best part is that it's all going to be off the grid."

"Really? Like no electricity and stuff."

"Solar power. And the houses will collect and filter rain water. My dad has all these books on it. Pretty neat, huh?"

"You think you can build just build a house? What about building codes and stuff."

"What? You've never heard of earthships, or strawbale, or cob houses? Seems like something you'd be into," she says.

I nod my head and look around, acting like I'm trying to picture it.

"Do you know what cob houses are?"

"I have no idea," I say.

"Cob," Erica says, "is basically mud and straw. You make softball size orbs of it and build up walls.

You get to sculpt your windows and doorways, the curve of each round wall. They're beautiful works of art, and you end up living in a hand-sculpted house made of the soil." She's beaming with excitement about this thing, but I'm picturing a mud hut in the wilderness.

"So you'll live like bushmen?" I laugh. "In mud huts, but in the California mountains?"

"I'll have to show you some pictures when we get back to town. They're beautiful homes, wonderfully natural, with circular walls and built in couches…you'll have to see pictures, Abbie. You'll love it."

I can see by her excitement that she is serious. So I decide to accept what she's saying, despite my inability to picture it. "I can't wait to see," I say, as sincerely as I can manage. "When is this going to happen?"

"That's the problem, I guess." Her tone drops back down to earth. "There really is no time line. They're very inexpensive to build. The roof is the only really expensive part. We've already dug a well, but that's about the only thing we've done out here."

"Well, like I said, I can't wait to see it."

I help Erica make camp, but I can hardly do a thing without her direction. I'm starting to feel kind of out of place. That feeling, mixed with Traveler's warning just gives me a feeling of unease. *Why did I come?* I just keep asking myself that. I had plenty of time to make up an excuse, and yet, here I am.

After moving around quite a bit and getting the fire started, it's feeling a lot warmer. I actually take off my sweatshirt and sit by the fire in just short sleeves.

"Tell me," Erica says as we sit by the fire. "What was your family's Winter Solstice like?"

I think back to my childhood. To when Mom was alive. "We haven't really celebrated it as a family since she died, you know?"

"Does your dad do Christmas?"

"I guess, kind of. We always mention that it is Christmas. But, since Mom died on Christmas, we've never had good associations with the actual day, or anything. We have some decorations and there are movies we like to watch."

"I didn't realize that was when she died."

"Yeah, Christmas morning. Lying in bed. Whispering something that none of us could make out." And now I feel rotten because Erica was trying to capture a light mood, not have me bring down the party. I stare into the fire, and once again, try and invoke memories of Mom. I take a deep breath. "But when she was alive, the Winter Solstice really was our biggest holiday."

"Yeah? Us too."

"We always had a Solstice feast. And we had a real tree that we had cut down ourselves, but very sparsely decorated. We would sit around the tree and talk about our year. We'd talk about what we had done to accomplish what we wanted to. Mom would make a speech about how important it was for us to embrace the dark side of life. How the dark side was part of the mystery of life and that this night, above all others, was time to indulge in the dark side of life and let it touch us.

"Then we would head out into the backyard where Dad would have built up a huge bonfire in the pit we used to have out there. We'd sit around the fire and sort of continue the discussion from inside. Talk about life and death and all the things that we know and don't know about the world and ourselves. Then, when the fire died down, we'd head inside and exchange just a few presents. We'd have hot chocolate and listen to quiet music. Things were less talkative after the bonfire.

"After that, we would sort of drift off in our own directions. I would go to my room and have a small ceremony of my own, usually involving dreaming. And they would go off and do their thing.

"What was your Solstice like?" I ask Erica.

"It was kind of similar. But we would have it up here, weather permitting. My extended family would come from all around, and we'd have the feast under the gazebo there. Everyone would bring something. It wasn't exactly like a Thanksgiving dinner, or anything, but it was good. Then we'd dance around the fire, under the moon. We'd sing and woop and dance. And, well, we'd do it skyclad."

"Skyclad? Really? In this temperature? With your *family*?"

"That's part of the whole positive attitude in the middle of life's darkness things that we do during the Solstice. Plus, I think my parents are total nudists."

"Oh god, how embarrassing."

"When I got older, and we got more and more involved with the coven, the coven started meeting up here. But then, other families would want to host. People didn't want to come all the way up here and all, and the parking sucks."

"Where is your coven now?"

"They're celebrating at some guy's ranch in Sanger. The coven meets there a lot. I never liked it as much when we started going to different places. I mean, the Solstice should really have snow. It should be cold, you know?"

"Yeah, I guess so," I say.

We go to the truck and pull out our coolers. We both brought food for our feast, which wasn't much of one. We cook hot dogs and smores and a pumpkin pie that I made just for the occasion. Erica has made wassail, the traditional wine of the Solstice. I have two helpings of it, despite my general aversion to alcohol; it tastes sweet and delicious. We finish eating just before dusk.

"Well? Shall we draw our circle?" Erica says.

"How do you draw a circle for two people out of doors?"

"Just look all around you. Take in all the land and the trees and the animals, and invite them all into your circle."

We both stand up and move our folding chairs away from the fire, so we can stand near it. Then, to my surprise, Erica begins taking off her clothes.

"Erica," I say. "God, do we *have* to?"

"*You* don't have to. But it's part of my tradition. It's very invigorating," she says, stripped down to her bra. I try not to watch as she peels off her jeans and then stands there pulling her bra off.

I know that I'll feel silly if I'm standing around in clothes while she goes nude. I don't want to feel like I'm not participating in the thrill of the moment. And maybe the wine was a little stronger than it tasted.

Hesitatingly, I start undressing. I throw the discarded garments onto my chair and hurry back to the fire to warm my naked body. I put my feet into my wool slippers. "Sorry if this isn't authentic enough! These shoes are staying on."

"Oh, for sure! The ground is freezing!" The firelight flickers across her curvy body and she looks like someone a Rubens would want to paint. "Goddess," she calls out. "Help us to face the mystery of life with faith and optimism. Help us not to shy away from the dark corners of our life. Help us to be at one with the nature where you have placed us. Let us feel your clock in our blood. Let us care for and honor this world you have made. And make us appreciate this brief life that you have loaned to us."

Inspired, I call out, "In the darkness, let us see your light. In your creations, let us see ourselves. In each other, let us find love and forgiveness. Breathe through us and let us feel your presence in all that we undertake. And give us the wisdom to enjoy our lives."

Again, my eyes meet Erica's across the fire, which seems to be burning brighter now. Suddenly, she draws in a breath and lets out an enormous *whoop*. I laugh and then respond with my own. Then she starts to sing *"The Holly and the Ivy,"* an ancient carol. I join her and we sway around the fire singing joyously. We sing the old songs that had been turned into Christmas carols. We dance, our bare feet against the rough bare ground. The cold that at first stings our body is chased away by our energy, our singing, our dancing, our happiness.

For the first time in my life, I feel the exuberance that the Solstice is supposed to be about. I feel that in the dead of winter, on the longest night of the year, the sun is being reborn in my heart, and that it is our celebration, our joy, our bravery in the face of the death of the world that is going to bring it back the next morning.

We stop our celebration only once, to have another cup of wassail. We stumble loudly over the words to the carol, *"Here We Come a Wassailing"* and laugh loudly at the weak grasp we have of the lyrics. I feel that this is the way the song was meant to be sung. Our voices echo off the trees, off the mountains, through the riverbeds and valleys. Our souls burn as brightly as the fire. We link arms and swing each other. The fire is the sun, we are the planets, and pure happiness is our life force.

It's late now, and the fire is dying a little low. Erica gathers wood, careful not to snag any rogue branches on her bare skin, and piles it on the fire. "We have to nurse the fire all night," she says. "To ensure that the sun comes back. I think we'll have enough wood, but we don't want it to get too low."

I don't have to tell her what a wonderful time I'm having. I don't have to tell her how beautiful the world is within this ceremony. Our eyes exchange this information freely; our smiles shine out as beacons to each other.

Without exchanging a word, we both go into the tent. I pull on my big flannel shirt that I wear as a nightgown on cold nights, but Erica just stays in her skin. We sit cross legged, facing each other. Erica unfolds an enormous blanket and drapes it over our shoulders.

"My grandmother was a member of The Losa tribe," she says. "She made this blanket for me when I was a teenager." The blanket is beautiful and covered with stars. It is strikingly warm for how light it feels on my shoulders.

"Did you bring your flute?" Erica asks.

"Yes," I say.

"Do you think you could try and take me into your dreaming? Try and show me how it's done?"

"Sure, let's try," I say. I reach into my bag and pull out my carved flute. It's wrapped in a silk scarf which I remove. I also pull out a cone of incense that I made, and a plate to put it on. I carefully light it with a match and set it to the far side of the tent, as far from the blanket as possible.

"Sit as comfortably as you can," I instruct. "Let your spine be straight and feel your body as it pushes down into the Earth. Feel the Earth push back on you, and feel this feeling as levity. Feel yourself being pushed up, lengthening your spine, lifting you up, floating. Listen to your breathing. Breathe in new, energetic air through your nose. Breathe out old, dry, dead air through your mouth. Feel what it is like to be here, now."

I wait a few minutes. I listen to my breathing. I feel the energy being replaced and renewed.

"Now," I say. "I'm going to play a note on the recorder. I want you to feel the note in you. Breathe it in. Resonate it. Let your spine ring at the same vibrations as the note. Let your body play the note back." I gently play a note with one long breath. Then I breathe in and do it again. I feel my blood course through the instrument. The instrument is not one of music, but of holy ritual. It is alive. It is a part of me. It is my connection to the world around me. And my connection to the many worlds underneath this one.

"I'm going to lower the note, now Erica. I'm going to lower your body; I'm going to move you down a full step." I play the lower note. I feel her sigh, as if she is letting out steam that was holding her up too high. I play through the note a few times more, making sure that she has enough time to feel it, to be the note.

Then I lower it again without saying a word.

And again.

And again.

We are low enough now, almost to the bottom of the register of my instrument. I've spent a long time doing this, much longer than I usually do for myself. Perhaps half an hour has passed. Gently, I step stand up, outside of my body. I look down at Erica, and it looks like she's ready to step out herself, but that she doesn't know it. I've never helped anyone out before, so I do it very hesitatingly.

I reach down under the sheet and gently touch her hand. I watch as her physical body twitches slightly. Then the eyes from her energy body open and look up at me.

"Slowly," I say. "As if you're stepping out of deep water. Stand up." I take her hand and help her out of her husk. She is naked before me, and I can't really tell if I'm wearing the flannel in this body or not, but I quickly try and blunt out the negativity. Now I don't have to talk anymore. I remember that thought is all you need to communicate, like when I was little and Mom showed this to me.

Let's go out and explore, I think.

She's frightened just a little, and very excited. She wonders if I'm certain that we're going to be able to get back in.

You can always get back in, I assure her with my mind. *The body will wait. The body will keep breathing. Now stop thinking about it, or you will end up there sooner than you would like.*

I'm there now, a little, she thinks.

It's normal to feel as if you're in two places at once, I try and tell her. *But be persistent. Orient yourself here.*

We walk out of the tent, and she is beaming with joy and excitement. This is really the first time that I've projected since Samhain. Well, not counting my times with Traveler. Though, I don't think I'm really projecting then. I don't know how that works.

Erica and I run there perimeter of the clearing. It's exuberating. Without thinking much of it, I leap into a tree and feel my body turn into the cat-like creature. I run and run, with the tunnel vision of a predator, before I hear Erica calling out for me.

I return to her and she looks frightened. She approaches me apprehensively.

Is that you? she thinks.

Don't worry, calm down, I send her. I didn't really mean to regress like that. But it feels *good.*

How? How do you do it? she wonders.

I try to put the feeling into thoughts. I try and explain to her that the body we see is the illusion of our earthly minds. I try to explain that, if we are at one with everything, we can take on any identity. That if she finds a creature, a totem, that she truly feels connected with, she can become it. It's not a transformation, like she may think, but instead it's just a different *interpretation* of the self. If you are at one with everything, you are at once yourself and a cat, so you can interpret yourself any way.

She's confused and I can see that she is drifting back to the tent. She'll wake up soon, I think, so I head back to the tent myself.

My energy is back in my body, and I open my eyes to see that Erica has fallen backwards, her arms outstretched, her breasts fallen to either side.

She opens her eyes.

"Oh, Gods!" she exclaims. "I've never had an

experience like that." She sits up. "Abbie, my gods, I can't thank you enough for that experience."

"It's my Solstice gift," I say, drowsily. The wassail is starting to make me very sleepy. "I didn't know what else to get you."

"It's the greatest gift ever," she says. "Do you think that I'll be able to do it myself? Without you?"

"Your body should remember. You may need to practice, but you should be able to do it. And don't worry about regressing down; you'll get the hang of that, too."

She talks and talks about it, going over the story of it again and again. I finally tell her that it's getting cold, and I have to go to sleep. We lie down, both covered by the blanket. In the dark, I can make out her face looking at mine. Her eyes are open and she is smiling gently. I reach out and brush her cheek with the back of my hand. She reaches up and holds my palm against her face.

Our legs are touching, they wrap in and around each other, seeking the warmth of the other's skin. I move my face forward, still holding her cheek, and at the last moment, I pull her face towards mine. We kiss, slowly. First, my lips are tense against hers, but they soften under her warmth. My lips part only slightly, at the same moment that hers do.

The kiss doesn't last long. The arc is small, and when it comes down, our faces separate. We smile at each other in the dark. We press our bodies together and the warmth makes me feel so welcome here.

"Good night, Abbie," Erica says sweetly. "Happy

Solstice."

"Good night, Erica," I say. "Happy Solstice." I fall asleep, glad to know that the sun will return in the morning.

Nineteen

Packing up camp was much harder work than setting up. The rather roomy tent has an oppressively small bag to fit in, along with all of its folded up supports and steaks. Folding and rolling the tent just right takes the better part of an hour and nearly sparks hostility between us. We sit by the still burning fire and cook bacon and eggs in a cast-iron skillet. They are probably the best bacon and eggs I've ever had. I drink as much water as I can, having a splitting headache from the wassail the night before. We talk quietly, huddled in jackets around our fire.

"So what's your family doing for Christmas?" Erica asks.

"They are gone to Mexico. Visiting sites of anthropological and philosophical interest."

"Wow. You didn't go?"

"No. I wasn't invited. Not expressly. I was expected, I think, to invite myself if I felt comfortable with that."

"It doesn't sounds like your dad."

"I think they're both frustrated with me. My dad thinks I need to find a job or really get back into schoolwork and apply myself or something productive."

"What do you think about that?" she asks.

"I don't know," I say. "I don't know which direction to point, you know? Everything is just so overwhelming. What do I want to do? You know? It's like everything is a choice and every choice has a right or wrong. Only none of them is actually right, just some are *less wrong*. I'm whining, I know."

"You'll figure it out, Abbie."

"Well, it sure as hell doesn't feel that way," I say. "And now," I say quietly, "I feel more confused than ever."

"Oh, Abbie. Don't be confused. Trust your path."

"What do you think I should do?" I ask her, looking into her face.

"What you want to."

"That's not a good enough answer for me."

"Abbie," she laughs. "I'm not going to make your decisions for you."

"No?"

"Of course not."

I'm looking at her and my eyes are asking what we should do about *us*. I don't know if our kiss meant anything, but I felt something. Did she?

"But I think you should at least *try* to do better in school, you know? The boring part is almost over, then there's college," she says, breaking our gaze. "You should major in something you love. Music. History. Whatever."

"Maybe," I say. "It just seems so…"

We stop talking for the rest of breakfast. After breakfast, we clean up everything we can and load everything into the truck. The last part of our Solstice ceremony is to dowse the fire. We make sure it is fully extinguished, no longer needing it in the light of day.

Except the day is cloudy. It's overcast and I'm afraid it will snow on us before we get back down to town. On the way back down, watching the landscape reverse itself from the day before, we don't talk about anything very important. We sing loudly to songs on the radio and fall apart in laughter when we realize that we only know half the lyrics to *Wide Open Spaces*, even though we sing it with the passion of two people singing an anthem.

Happy and silly, the hour and thirty minutes it takes to get back down to town. At one point, after laughing hard, Erica rests her hand on my knee. It lingers there a little long, and she rubs my leg for a moment or two. That is the only part of today that is anything like last night.

I close my eyes and remember the night before. My body wrapped up with hers under the blanket was the warmest mid-winter night I've ever spent.

Twenty

Mom never took me to where she grew up.

I always used to wonder why. Dad grew up in San Francisco, and we spent ages touring the city. My family traveled to San Francisco every chance we had. My dad showed us the house where he grew up, where he went to school, where his dad worked. We ate in his favorite restaurants. We trod, with reverance, the path of his childhood.

And in doing this, I felt connected to my dad. I felt like I knew a side of him that gave me a glimpse into who he is now. It's a lot like how I like to read historical fiction. I felt like I was a part of his whole life. And that he was proud of that.

But we never did the same for Mom.

She grew up in Pacific Grove, near Monterey. It's just 100 miles south of San Francisco, and only a couple hours away from Ashlan. But we never ever went there. I always heard it was a pretty place, and once in a while Mom would talk about it. She always talked about growing up, about her mom, about her upbringing, but she very rarely put it in a place. I always wondered why.

Right after I turned sixteen, Vic and I drove to Pacific Grove. I told Dad that we were going to a concert in San Jose, and felt badly about the lie. Really, I wasn't even sure *why* I lied. I just figured that there was a secret about the place that I wasn't supposed to know. Although it was never said, I just kind of thought that the town was off-limits to me. So we snuck there.

I picked up Vic, who did not yet have his license (his parents were withholding the test from him as disciplinary action for I can't remember what), in my Volvo which was so new to me back then. Vic had been to Monterey several times, and he said that there was nothing there that I was going to find. There was no secret written in the waves that would tell me what my mom was like when she was there.

Driving into Monterey, there's a wonderful moment, coming over a hill, where the sea air hits you in the face. And a moment after that air hits you, off in the distance, you see the ocean spread out in front of you. To either side of you are expanses of land that's used for farming, or are not used at all. It looks like the road is going to go on right into the ocean, when it curves south and follows the coast down to Monterey.

On the north end of town is the old army base, Ft. Ord. In its shell is now a college, where a couple of friends of mine want to go. It was the army that brought my mom's family to the area in the first place. Heading south, you cross some dunes, hug the coast, and come to Monterey. We spent a good deal of time looking around the touristy old street of Canary Row, and saw monument after monument to John Steinbeck. Then we went on to the fisherman's wharf, where ships leave on whale watching tours and every restaurant insists that you try a paper cup of their chowder.

All along the way, I kept trying to imagine my mom. I tried to see her there. I tried to *feel* her there. I tried to place her there. But it was looking more and more like Vic was right; there wasn't a secret. There was a place. And whatever my mom had to do with it was invisible to me now. And I wondered the whole time if maybe it would have been invisible to her, coming back after all these years.

We made it to the very small town of Pacific Grove right after lunch. We walked in to the library and I paged through the old phone books, looking for my grandfather's name. We finally found the address, on Lighthouse, and drove down to find the house.

Lighthouse is a beautiful old street, full of old Victorianish houses overlooking the ocean, at times. The road curves up and down, and it was at one of these crests that we found my mother's house. Disappointingly, it looked like it was just then being built.

I talked to one of the construction workers and he explained to me that the original house had been torn down and that this new one was being built. It was tall, this new building, and almost all windows facing the ocean. It was square, boxy, and modern. Alongside the older houses, this one was a travesty. Like when a restaurant goes out of business and a McDonald's takes its place. It didn't have the charm of Pacific Grove.

The house behind it, facing the other way, struck me as the prettiest house that I had ever seen. It was tall, three stories, but old and mangled by the weather. It looked unoccupied, had a for sale sign on it. The new house, where Mom's used to be, looked like it blocked any view this house may have had of the ocean. And besides that, it didn't look inhabitable.

The windows were broken out. The middle of the house sagged down towards the center—a sure sign of a very poor foundation on a shifting hill by the ocean. The sides were crumbling off in chunks, and the roof was so full of holes, you could see inside the attic at places. It reminded me of the old mill in that one Disney cartoon.

But you could tell that once it was an amazing house. The stone work that framed the windows and doors was designed to make this house look regal and imposing. The wall around the yard was made of the same dark stone, and it had a stone gargoyle-like cat crawling along it just at the gate. The porch, made of wood, was carved with all kinds of shapes. The handrails and the banister along were hand carved into angles and flowers.

I hopped the low wall and walked across the small, overgrown lawn, and ran my hands along the carvings on the porch. I turned over my shoulder to Vic, "This is it, Vic," I said. "This is where my mom's bed comes from."

"What are you talking about?"

"You know, the bed that's in the guest room? The really cool one? The same person who made that bed carved this porch."

"Abbie," Vic said, leaping the fence and coming over to join me. "No one carves a porch."

"This one is carved. And I swear it's the same carver. I can just tell. Everything about it is identical. God, I wish we had a camera."

On the drive home, Vic conceded that it wasn't out of the question that the bed comes from the house behind where my mom's was. "But what does that do for us? What have you learned from coming all the way out here with me?"

"I don't know yet," I answered. "But I've always known that her bed was a one-of-a-kind, but I've never known much beyond that."

"How does that show you anything?"

"I don't know," I said. "It's just one tiny piece of the puzzle. One tiny bit of my mom's past. An answer to one small question."

"A question that is hardly worth the bother to ask."

"Right."

I never told my dad about it. I tried to look up some kind of information about the house, but beyond seeing the absurdly high price the property was going for, I didn't learn anything else. I eventually just let the whole thing drop. But now that Traveler is back, it's not surprising that I would start to rehash these demons.

Sol Smith

Twenty-One

It is another Thursday night, and I am getting home from another show at Stones. Vic's band was really on this time. They had two new songs from the week before, and they sounded as polished as ever. They were in talks, I heard, with a producer from LA who was looking to find new talent. He had just signed a band up in Modesto, gave them a pretty nice deal, and one of the band members used to play with The Discounted. So he tipped off the producer, and the rumor was that the producer was going to be there tonight. So that might explain why they played so damn well.

During their break, Vic came over and sat with us at our table. Erica, Derek, and I wanted to hear his thoughts on the rumor about the producer.

"I don't know; this is the first I'm hearing of it," he said.

"Bullshit," I said. "Everyone's been talking about it. There's no way that you haven't heard."

"I really haven't. Those guys up in Modesto got lucky. It doesn't take talent, it doesn't take skill, you just have to be doing the right thing at the right time.

It's not a question of how good you are - just listen to the radio."

"Good point," Derek said. "But that doesn't change the fact that all this isn't news to you. You're either a liar, or there's someone here you're trying to impress."

"It sure as hell isn't you, bro," Vic said. "I haven't heard a word about it."

We sit there and talk a while longer before Derek has to go home.

"You want to slip out?" Vic says to me.

"What do you mean?"

"You know, go for a walk or something?"

"Vic, it's cold out, what's wrong with sitting here?"

He looks around at the other tables. "There's not a lot of privacy here."

I put on my coat and hat and Vic and I walk over to the old Mission. We sit down on the steps and look at the soft white lights that have been strung all over the square for Christmas. In the fog, the small lights have soft halos around them. In my coat, I'm still cold, but Vic reaches his arm around me.

"About what everyone was saying," he says out of the blue. "About us playing better."

"Yeah?"

"I think it's *you*, Abbie."

I pull back and look at him in disbelief. "Me?"

"Yeah, you know, since you've been coming again and all. I just feel this different electricity from the audience; from you."

First he plays down his excitement about this agent rumor, and now he's treating me like I'm his muse. And this is totally unlike him. I smile at him, but in a kind of frown way, like I feel sorry for him. And I do feel sorry. I feel kind of like I am turning him into someone he's not.

Stepping in the door, I can tell that Dad and Teri are asleep. The house is quiet and dark. I am home pretty late and don't want to draw any attention to myself. I creep up the stairs and they creek and moan with every single step I take.

Ever since Dad and Teri got back from Mexico, I've hated walking up the stairs at night. They bought these totally macabre pictures from a shop in Mexico. It used to be a tradition in the 19th century for families in Mexico to take once last picture with their deceased relative. They would prop them up in their coffins; dads and moms and daughters and grandpas in their coffins and the rest of the family would gather around for the shot. The dead ones are dressed in their finest, with their hands folded neatly in front of them. And on their face is that grim smile of death; the muscles hardened, the face contorted, and what's left is a stretched mouth with the teeth clasped together tight, every tooth showing to the camera.

It's also an unfortunate side effect of the photography of the day that the lens had to remain open so long to take a decent picture. Because of that, the people surrounding the dead have moved or jostled, ending up ever-so-slightly out of focus, while the dead remain still and are in sharp clarity.

I walk up the stairs trying not to look at or think of these pictures. Why they would put things like this up on the wall, is beyond me. I get to the top of the staircase, and I am startled to see my own reflection staring back at me. Teri has been rearranging things, and this mirror, which did hang in guest room, now hangs on the top of the stairs.

"It lifts the eye," she said when she moved it, "lets you appreciate the full height of the ceiling." She's such a snot. Instead of appreciating anything, however, I let out a stunted and smothered scream. Right on cue, I see the light in my dad's room turn on. Before I can get to my room, Dad is out of his room and standing in the hallway.

"Are you okay, honey?"

"Yeah," I say. "I just saw that damn mirror again."

"You're out pretty late, don't you think?"

"I was having a good time, Daddy. I'm sorry. Time just got away."

"Abigail, let's talk," I can see his outline, but I can't make out his face. "In your room. Just a couple minutes. I want to turn the light off for Teri."

"Time isn't even a thing, Dad. Maybe don't sweat it."

"Just a minute, you can talk!"

I go into my room and lie down on bed. I'm tired. Really, really tired. I'm afraid that I'm going to fall asleep before Dad comes in. When he finally does, I gaze at him with a look that's supposed to communicate, *"can't this wait?"*

"Honey," he says. "I've been meaning to talk to you for a while."

"What about, Dad?"

"Teri. I'm getting the impression that you don't get along with her as much as you would like." This is my dad talking. An absolute genius with sentence structure. Here is he trying to get me to be more accepting of Teri, and he's wording it like it's my idea. He's disarming me completely.

"It's not that I don't want to get along with her, Dad," I say, ignoring the suggestion of his syntax. "I'm just feeling left out. I'm not as big a part of your life anymore, you know?"

"No, that's not true. You're every bit a part of my life. It's just that our relationship has to change. We have to start to understand each other at a new level. Remember when we talked about what you wanted to do, with a job or school?"

"Yes, Daddy, I remember."

"This all goes with that. This is all part of growing up."

"I know about growing up, Dad, come on, I'm so sleepy."

"I don't know that you do," he says in a very un-condescending way. "It's a process that doesn't end. It's a process that goes on and on, no matter what age you are."

"Dad, no offense, but my eyelids are, like, closing here, you know? It's not that I'm bored. It's that I have no idea what to focus on and I'm sleepy. Please, please, skip to your thesis, okay?"

"Teri and I are getting married."

I want to say, *big deal, Dad, you're practically married anyway.* But instead of anything rational, or anything snide, I start to tear-up. I hold back from sobbing by looking away from Dad. He sits down on the bed and wraps his arms around me.

Dad and I talk a little while longer, but I honestly don't really retain any of it. Those words about marriage just keep bouncing around in my ears. And I can see him talking and see that he's smiling, but nothing is registering. And I don't know if I'm smiling or nodding, or what, because all I can think about is a few minutes in the past.

Finally, Dad stands up and walks out of the room. He walks into the darkness of the hallway, and I feel like I might as well be watching him walk away from me forever. He's disappearing, just like Mom did, and I'm left sitting here alone. I can hear his steps down the hall, and finally his door closing. It's not like I thought that things between Dad and Teri were going to end, but it's not like I didn't somehow hope that things were going to go back to how they were, too.

The shadows of leaves fill my room, swaying in the breeze. I watch their flow and I feel like I'm one of them. I'm just drifting in a tide that I didn't make. I'm just sitting on a branch at the mercy of this much bigger being, in this much bigger world, and something as soft and invisible as the wind can blow me around and make me fall.

Every person I know has more power over me than I do. My dad, Teri, Erica, Vic, whoever. They all have the ability to shake the branch, rock the tree, and send me tumbling to the ground. And they don't even know it.

And they don't even care.

Twenty-Two

"Poor Abbie," Traveler says. "You must have known that this was going to happen."

"Of course I did," I say. "But I had no idea I'd be so broken up about it."

"I guess you never can know how you'll be affected."

Traveler sits patiently and holds me for a while. Ever since I was young, ever since Mom died, I've tried not to cry. I can't stand feeling this out of control; this vulnerable. It's torturous to have your emotions spill out of you so literally.

"What can we do, Traveler?" I ask her when I've finished sobbing.

"Honey," she says motherly. "You don't want to change your dad's plans. You don't want to get in the way of his happiness. You know how much better he's been since he's been with her. No matter what you do, no matter what kind of good friend and caretaker you've been to your dad, you can never do for him what Teri has. Never."

"Where does that leave me?"

Traveler wipes the tears from my face with the

sheets. "It leaves you with me, for one. And, pretty soon, it leaves you with Vic. It's okay to be sad, Abbie, but don't indulge in it too long. We have to be strong and stand up to these forces if you want to gain control again."

God, the idea of 'gaining control' sounds so goddamn draining, you know? I'm grateful for Traveler. I'm grateful for how she's been helping me to get Vic. But I'm still not sure that's what I want. I'm still not sure who I see myself with. Or if I see myself with anyone. And there was that moment with Erica which made me wonder about things even more. And putting out the effort to even try, all of a sudden, seems impossible.

Traveler senses my hesitance. "Honey," she says. "You're in a strange place. You're very confused. And vulnerable."

"I know."

"It's not healthy for you to be making huge decisions right now."

"Like the decision to be with Vic." I say.

"Exactly. You can't see the forest for the trees, honey. You need to trust that I have a pretty good picture of what's going on in your life. You've never mentioned it, but I know what has happened between you and Erica."

"I thought you would know."

"And I'm not upset with you."

"You can be upset with me if you want, Traveler, I don't care. You warned me that my energy would be sapped and I'm really feeling that crash now. I know that you knew about the whole thing. I just don't have the energy anymore, Traveler. I just want to sleep and keep on sleeping, you know?"

Traveler is playing the perfect patient mother. She takes a few breaths and backs up just a little from me, giving me a little more of my own space. "Abigail," she says. "I'm here to help you. I told you that Erica had an enchantment on you. I just really wasn't sure what kind it was."

"You think Erica has me in a love spell?"

"I'm not sure. I'm not trying to levy accusations here."

"Traveler," I say, calmly. "Erica hasn't tried anything since then. She's been a perfect lady around me. I think that both of us aren't sure what exactly that was about. I think both of us don't know what to do, if anything, about the situation. We haven't even talked about it, not even once. And it's been almost a month."

"Just the same, Abigail. I can see how bothered you are when we talk about Erica. So I'll tell you what: we won't talk about her. I'll let you sort out your friends yourself. But, if you want to get things going again, if you want to feel like you're in control, you have to control the situation between Vic and you. After that, you can be with Erica, or with whoever you want, it won't matter. But you need to get your energy back from Vic."

I stand up and walk to the window. I sit down on the cedar chest. "I can't do it, Traveler. I told you that I can't. It's just too hard, too draining, and too weird. I'm not into it."

"When you are treated like a conquest, Abbie, the predator walks away with a part of you. You are incomplete without getting that part back. You have to prove that you are an empowered person. This kind of defeat would be fine for a normal person. But if you want to be an accomplished witch, like Mom was, you will take care of this situation. You will win him back. After that, see what I care. Dump the guy. Whatever you want."

I am wounded by Traveler's tone. She's losing patience with me, and I feel so wrapped up in this thing that I don't know which way is up anymore. "Traveler," I say. "I love you and I trust you. But I feel like getting *out* of *all* these situations. I can't handle this kind of pressure. Let's just slip away, start over. I can't face all of this without even Dad around for me anymore, you know?"

"You can't handle it because you're incomplete. But it has to be done, Abigail. I can't let you lie around and act defeated. Pull yourself up. So Dad's getting married, big deal. So you kissed a girl, get over it, you're not the first. Vic's not far off now, you've made lots of headway. Just get over all this bullshit and step up, Abigail."

"Can't you just do it for me?"

Traveler laughs. Then she stops. Her face goes from smiling to serious. "Maybe, Abbie. There may be a way I could do it for you."

"How?"

"Hold on." Traveler stands up and walks into the closet. She comes out with a large, tattered book in her hands. "This is my grimmerie," she says.

"Where did it come from?" I ask.

"It's ages older than our family's other one, Abbie. This one goes *way* back."

Again, I start to wonder about Traveler. I start to wonder what the hell she is, really.

"There may be something in here that can help us." Traveler sits down on her bed and starts very carefully thumbing through the pages. I sit down next to her and look over her shoulder at the book.

I've never seen anything like it. It's strange and complicated. The words are unreadable to me, in some distant language. There are charts and symbols that are hand-drawn, and they don't make a lot of sense to me either.

"Here it is," she says. "This spell will make it so my will can work directly through you." She points as a page that is just as garbled and strange to me as any of the others. "I'm going to have to cast it from this side, with your help."

"Why from your side?" I ask.

"There are ingredients here that are unavailable to you," she says. "But, like I said, I need your help to do it. I'll need you to bring yourself pretty low so you can hold things from my world." I reach my hand to her book and find nothing but air. "See? It can't be done by just me."

"You're going to need a lot of energy," Traveler continues. "Remember how you were drained and tired after casting the love spell? This is going to be much more draining."

"Can't I just do some regressing and get energy that way?"

"No, this has to be physical energy gained in your physical world. Your body is going to go through a lot with this spell."

"Should I be scared?"

Traveler smiles, "Not at all, Abigail. We're just going to put me with you for a while, a couple days, and I will take care of you on these crossroads. You'll get some rest, and when you get back into things, you'll feel better than ever."

It sounds so good. Traveler, I know, is going to do a better job of taking care of me than I will. And the chance to just rest is hopeful beyond anything else I can imagine right now.

"I have some instructions for you," she says.

Traveler shows me some exercises to do. They're some kind of mix between calisthenics and yoga. She says that they will help me build up a surplus of energy in my body and in my organs—energy collected from the energy of the Earth. Then she shows me how to sun gaze. She shows me to sit facing the sun at a 45-degree angle and to flash my eyes at it in such a way that the light reflects off of the inside of my lenses. This, she says, is so full of energy that it borders on the nutritious; there are witches who sun gaze instead of having meals at certain holy times.

I practice these things religiously. And for the next few nights, I don't see Traveler at all. She told me that she would be away for a little while, making sure all was ready for this spell. She is so excited that I came up with the idea for this that she can hardly contain herself. In the meantime, I try to stay at home as much as possible. I only really leave the house to play on Sunday night.

And when I'm playing, I see Erica sitting there, in the front row, listening to my music and my words. I sing a song about her, about our Solstice together. I don't think she knows that's what it's about. But when I sing it and I look at her face, I can see a part of me that is hard to recognize. I decide to get Traveler's word that she will get Vic for me, but not distance me from Erica.

Just in case.

Twenty-Three

It's fifteen minutes till midnight. I draw my circle and sit in a chair in the middle of it. I light two white candles and two black candles. I ask for the help of the gods. I ask for the power to do this. I can feel new energy coursing through my body from the exercises Traveler showed me. I feel like I can run a marathon.

The moon is new tonight, and the light in the room is dim without the candles.

I sit in my seat and bring my cello up into position. I can feel its wooden body against mine, and I hear Traveler's words coming back to me. She told me the cello would do better for this ceremony. She told me that the cello has a closer resonance to the human body. That I will be able to match it better. That I will be able to go lower.

Just in case, she told me to tune the bottom string down to an F. That way I can lower it and lower it without feeling like I'm running out of room.

The cello is in tune. When the strings are in tune with themselves, the instrument feels lighter, as if the overtones will grant it levity.

I take a deep breath and, as I let it out, I pull the bow across the string. My right hand holds the bow, and I can feel the string through the hairs and through the wood. My left hand holds the string, and I can feel it vibrating, wanting to get away from me. I hold it still, and shake my hand slowly, back and forth, back and forth, to give it a pleasing vibrato.

It sounds beautiful in this space.

It fills the room.

It fills my body.

I lower the note, and without breaking the sound, I push the bow onto the new and lower note. I feel my body drop lower. My body feels the vibrato. My body resonates the tone along with the body of the cello. I can feel my heartbeat go lower.

This sensation, this feeling of descent is a thousand times more vivid than when I play my flute. I can't believe I've never thought of this before. I feel like my physical body is phasing out of this world, as I get a fifth lower than where I started.

I resist the urge to play the notes higher. I imagine what it would feel like to make the notes soar to the top of the fingerboard, to make the cello sing me into a higher plane of existence.

Instead I move lower. And lower, and lower. And the energy that I felt at the beginning, the marathon running energy that coursed through my veins, is all but gone. I can hardly hold my bow up, I can hardly press my finger against the string. I open my eyes and I can see Traveler's face superimposed against the wall behind her.

"Keep pushing, Abbie," I hear her as if in a whisper. "Keep going, I can almost help you."

And just before I am so weak that the bow falls out of my hand, Traveler reaches over and helps me to hold it up. "There," she says, "Right now we're in almost the same place."

I can say nothing in return.

Her fingers help mine press against the string, rocking out the vibrato. And as I move one note lower, I feel like I'm not helping at all anymore. Like Traveler is holding the bow up, Traveler is holding me up.

"Okay, Abbie," she says. "Let go of the instrument, and move yourself off of the chair."

I do what I am told and I slump to the floor. Traveler takes the seat behind me and she is now holding the cello.

"That is *perfect*, Abbie," she says excitedly, though still quietly. "Now is where we shift things just a little."

I can't quite remember, but I was almost to the lowest note that my cello would play.

But now, Traveler, cello in hand, slowly moves the note one half-step higher. "Oh, yes," she says. "Just perfect, Abbie." And she moves it higher. And higher. Soon she's on the next string, and I struggle to sit up and try and make sense of what she is doing.

As she moves higher, and higher, everything around me gets dimmer and dimmer. I can see only by the light of the black candles. The white ones have gone almost completely out, and I am watching Traveler play my mother's cello, sitting in the chair where I started. I am seeing her in black-and-white, almost.

The cello gets higher, and it is almost to the note where I started. Then she stops playing entirely.

"What happened," I say, but it's a struggle to say anything.

Traveler doesn't look like she heard me. She stands up and rests the cello down on the ground. Then she stands up straight and looks straight ahead of her. "Thank you, Goddess, for helping us through this difficult task. This circle is broken." And she blows out the candles.

Without the aid of the candles, I can only see by a light that seems to be emanating from Traveler's body. Nothing else is lit up in the room at all, even when she goes and turns on the light switch.

"Abbie," she says out loud, but not to me or to any specific direction. "If this worked alright, then you can hear me. Thank you, Abbie. I cannot tell you how wonderful it feels to be whole again." She leaves the door and shuts it behind her. All I can see, feel, or hear is dark. I don't even know if I'm still there.

Then I notice a very tiny light where the window should be.

Part III—The Burning of Witch

Twenty-Four

I've been practicing what Abbie showed me in the mountains on Yule for weeks now. It hasn't worked really well, but I haven't given up. I went to a music store and bought an alto recorder, which was about the size of the flute that Abbie had made. I never really played an instrument before, so it took some practice to play even a simple note. My fingers hardly cover up the dumb holes, but I figure it out okay after a while.

Most of the time, when I did manage to play everything right, I would end up falling asleep in my circle, rather than being able to project. I think what finally pushed things over the edge and made me successful was when Abbie told me the proper incense to use and tea to drink. The combination worked wonders, and I was able to leave my body three times in as many days.

Now, as I step out of my body and look at it slumped over in the chair, I think that it's time to really concentrate on the regression. Earlier in the week, I was able to start the process of changing into, well, *something* before the guy from down the hall knocked on my door and woke me up out of my trance. The next time I tried, I got overly excited, lost concentration, and ended up waking up in my physical self again.

The time that I started to change, I think I was changing into some kind of bird. That's a happy thing for me, since I love birds, have always loved to watch them, and I treasure the idea of flying. So after giving it tons and tons of thought while awake, I have decided that the best way to ensure a full and quick transformation—or reinterpretation—is to leap out of my window.

My apartment isn't too high up. I'm on the second floor. But a leap even from this height would break my neck for sure. That puts some fear in me even though I'm not in my physical self and nothing would happen to me even if I did fall. I just feel like the urgency of not falling will help motivate me to turn into a bird. It's not how Abbie showed me, but I think it will work.

I stand here looking out at the sidewalk beneath me. I'm standing full height on my window sill, holding on to the roof with my right hand for balance. It's so funny, like I need any balance when there are no discernable rules of physics in this state of being. It just goes to show you how unbelievably and stupidly stuck in our ways we are.

I jump out, and before hitting the ground, I feel the shift within me. The wind speeds under my new wings and I am flapping up to a higher altitude. It's an exhilarating feeling, being a bird, flying, collecting and borrowing the energy from the world around me. I flap up high and look down on the trees in the neighborhood. Unlike my usual dreaming, I have no problem at all keeping my attention and fully experiencing this world.

It's late at night, for sure after midnight, so I think that I should go and see Abigail. She could be sleeping and maybe I can contact her. Or maybe she's doing a dreaming session right now. She'll be so proud to see me, and I guess she'll be able to tell me what kind of bird I am.

I feel like something powerful. I can feel how I pound the air out from under my wings and I don't know how fast I'm going, but I rarely see any birds go this fast, I'm sure.

Abbie's house is just a few blocks away, and I don't have any trouble recognizing it from up high and in the dark. I fly up to Abbie's window, which of course is wide open, and I peek inside.

A girl who looks to be about our age is sitting close to Abbie, who is playing the cello very slowly. They are surrounded by candles which are lit, and I think it must be some kind of ceremony that they are having. The girl reaches up to Abbie's fingers and helps her drag the bow across the strings. Her other hand is holding down the strings on the cello where Abbie's hand has slumped off and is hanging by her side.

The girl stands up and moves almost behind Abigail, who is dropping her head like she's falling asleep in algebra. The girl keeps one hand on the fingerboard and she takes the bow right from under

Abbie's grasp. I could swear that she puts her right hand right *through* Abbie's hand when she takes the bow. She gives Abbie just a slight shove, and then takes her seat on the chair. Abbie collapses and lies like a pile of laundry on the floor.

The girl looks much brighter and more vivid than she did before. She looks like she's experiencing a sudden burst in energy, and she's thrilled, happy, joyous to be doing this. The strange girl stands up and rests the cello on its side. She says something happily to Abigail and then she runs out of the room.

Abbie looks like she's not feeling very well. She stumbles and struggles over to her bed. She is faded of color. She looks like she's coming in on an old TV set with bad reception.

"Abbie," I call out. "What's going on?"

From her bed, Abbie is sitting up and squinting hard at me. "Who is that?"

"It's me, Abbie," I say. "It's Erica." I fly over and perch on the footboard of the bed. "Can you see me? What do I look like?"

Abbie is looking right at me, but she looks like she can hardly see me. "You're a finch, Erica. How funny. What a tiny finch you are. I'm sorry, Erica," she goes on, "but I'm not sure what's happening to me. I can see you, and I can see *that* it's you, but you're pretty much all I can see. Why is it so dark in here?"

"It's not that dark, Abbie. Are you okay? You don't look well."

"I don't think so."

"Who was that? The girl who just left?"

"That was my big sister, Erica. It's Traveler."

I am taken aback by this. "I didn't know you had a sister, Abbie."

"Please, Erica, I can't explain right now. She's not real, or maybe she is. I don't know. Please don't make me tell you all about it right now. Just go and get her and tell her that I don't want to do this anymore. Tell her I want to switch back. I can't stay here, I just can't. I thought this would feel different."

"Abbie, are you okay?"

"No, Erica, I'm not. I don't know what's happening to me. I need to get some rest." She puts her head down on the bed and starts to cry. "For god's sake, Erica, go find Traveler and tell her that I don't want this anymore."

I find Traveler walking down the street towards Mission Square. She's walking at a fast pace, almost skipping along, and she's humming. I fly around her trying to get the strange girl's attention, but it doesn't work. Of course she can't see me, I think to myself, she's not in dreaming. And how much time do I really have left before I lose it and wake up? So I fly back to Abbie's house, where I find her balled up in bed.

When I fly back in, she looks right at me. "Erica?" she says. "How long were you gone?"

"I don't know, exactly. Five minutes or less."

"I had no idea how long you were gone."

"Well, I'm here now, Abbie. Don't worry."

"I don't understand what's happening. You're all I can see. Everything else is black, but you're sitting here and you look like a small luminous bird. I can see the bed, a little, but that's it. What is happening?"

"I guess I am a bird. I regressed down. For the very first time."

"You're in the dream state?"

"Yeah, I used the method you told me about. Now what the hell is going on with you? You're in dreaming, too, right?"

"No. Well, no. Not exactly," Abbie says.

Abigail tells me all about her older sister. She tells me, but I have to say that not only does it take everything I've got to stay in the dream state that long, but I have a really hard time believing what she has to say. I start to think that this is nothing but a very, very vivid dream.

"Why haven't you told me about this before?"

Abigail shakes her head. "You're kidding, right? What would you have thought if I told you I was spending vast amounts of time with my imaginary friend?"

"It doesn't look like she's so imaginary," I say. "How long do you think this spell will last?"

"How long has it been? I have absolutely no sense of time. It feels like it might have been hundreds of years already, or like it never happened."

"It hasn't been long. I can't stay in dreaming very long."

"You're going to have to learn how to stay in it much longer," Abbie tells me. "I can't stand to spend time alone here."

"You're not going to have a lot of a choice, Abbie.

I really hate to leave you, but I'm going to have to. I'm going to have to wake up and go talk to this Traveler."

Abbie looks heartbroken at the idea. "I don't know what I'm going to do here, Erica."

"You're going to keep your wits, is what you're going to do. Remember, the first law of Wicca is to know yourself. This is a good time to get to know the new you. Try and find out your limitations here, what you can and can't do. I'll come visit and give you an update whenever I can."

I fly out the window, and without having to fly all the way back home, I suddenly awake, sitting in the middle of my circle. I remember the events vividly, but regardless, I go through my ritual of writing down every single detail I can remember in my dream journal. Then I rush out the door to try and find out how true all of it was.

Twenty-Five

I can't believe how sad I am to see Erica fly out of my room.

The darkness doesn't so much surround me as go in and out of me. I mistake this blackness for myself. I have no idea at times where or who I am, then, suddenly, I will think something resembling a thought, and mistake the voice of that thought for someone else. I begin to get excited, thinking I have company again, but I soon realize it was nothing more than my desire for company I heard. And by the time that thought has reached its completion, I've lost track of what it was I was thinking about.

While Erica was here, I was much better placed in time. I felt much closer to normal. I could keep perfect track of our conversation. She glowed a little, and lit part of the room around her like a faint night light. I imagine this must be what I looked like to Traveler.

I suppose "look" is the wrong word to use. I'm certainly not seeing with eyes. I'm perceiving something that isn't altogether different from vision, but it's on a much more subjective scale. Instead of seeing, it's like a *knowing*, but I knowing that is somehow incorporated with the idea of thought. Or that's how I'm interpreting it.

"I've always been different," I hear myself think, "but it is strange not being human anymore."

I ponder the idea of what it is to be human or to not be human. I get lost in the thought and begin to explore the darkness. It's hard for me to understand what the limits of my being exactly are. I don't know if I have a definite shape or not. I don't know if I fade out at the edges like a cloud, of it I am a set, finite creature. It's all very confusing. But I feel somehow bound to the bed; part of the bed. And Traveler stood and walked away; solid and human. And though I remember Erica's remark about trying to understand myself, I don't get much further than feeling one hand with the other and counting them, then taking them apart and trying to decide if they're still there or not.

I've overcome with sadness as I remember how wonderful it was to be able to know how many hands I had at what time. Something about that simple distinction seems so luxurious to me all of a sudden. I call out, in as close to and auditory call as possible, "Mom, if you can hear me, I need you."

I'm not sure how much time passes, ages or minutes, and I feel a hand on my left one. I put my right hand on top of the two others and count. Then I remove it and count again. As near as I can figure, I still have two hands, but there is another one holding my left hand. I imagine this must be the hand of the darkness itself, then I touch and count again.

Twenty-Six

I miss Abbie so much.

By the time I caught up with Traveler that first night, she was sitting in Stone's with Vic, having a drink. She was happy, radiantly happy, and Vic was talking to her like she was no stranger, but that they had been friends for years. When they saw me, they called me over for a drink. They seemed to think that this was the way it should be, that is was how it always was.

I couldn't think of doing something like confronting her right there. It was all too strange. I decided that it was probably best to bide my time and let her think that I suspected nothing. Under the conditions, it seemed like the only decision to make if I wanted to remain safely out of a mental hospital, able to somehow figure out a way to help Abigail.

It's strange watching this girl. Everyone seems to think she's been here all along. Traveler seems to have not only adopted Abbie's life, but replaced it. I seem to be the only one who remembers Abbie even exists. I explained this to Abbie a few nights ago, and she seemed to understand the concept very well.

"Erica, I can hardly remember existing myself," she told me in her room while Traveler was still out. I tried to keep eye contact with Abbie, even though her glowing green eyes are so full of hurt and sorrow. "My whole life seems like something I imagined, or something that I dreamed. And little by little it's slipping away. I can tell that if I'm here for too long, I'll no longer have any way to remember what I was like or who I was. You have to keep reminding me, Erica."

"Everyone calls her Traveler," I told her. "They seem to see her as she is. She has your old eyes, the brown ones. She's stepped right in to your old friends. She hangs on Vic like he's her moon and sun. I haven't heard one of them say they're dating, but they must be, don't you think?"

Abbie's down-turned face didn't change or react to that. I was afraid she would be even more hurt by that news.

"I know," she said at last. "They were here the other night."

"Oh, gods, Abbie," I said in a consoling tone. "I'm so sorry you had to see it."

"Any time anyone comes in here is a happy time, Erica. The room is illuminated with the burning of their lives. And my god does Vic burn brightly."

"I've always thought that."

"You have no idea. He beams his life in all directions like nothing I've ever seen. It's no wonder he's so attractive to people."

I tried to imagine the faint glow that I emit, still a

small bird in my dreaming. "Did they," I said slowly, "*do* anything?"

Abbie let out something close to a sigh. "No, they talked, they laughed. Lots of touching. But no."

I was so sorry to hear it. I knew it had to hurt her in so many ways to watch. I had to change the subject. "She's been very sweet to me, Abbie," I said lamely.

"I told her to."

"What?"

"I made her promise not to push you away. I said to bring Vic in if that's what she wanted in my life, but I made her swear not to push you away." Abigail said this heavily, sadly. "I didn't get the impression that she liked you, when I was alive."

"Any luck communicating with her?" I asked.

"Not yet, no. She either doesn't hear me, or she's faking."

"Why would she fake?" I asked.

"*Why* is a word that runs through my head all the time, Erica."

Now I sit at a table at Stones, watching Vic's band play, sitting at a table with Traveler and Derek. It's so unnerving sitting with this abomination, trying to act like it was her I knew all along. Like it was *her* that I went to garage sales with. Like it was *her* who spent the Solstice with me. Like it was my attraction to *her* that kept me up night after night.

It's been almost two months since Abbie has disappeared in everyone's mind and this beast has replaced her. She seems to have no idea that I share her secret, and for that I am unendingly glad. If only I can stay close enough to her and try to find a way to get things reversed.

The most frightening times are when I stop thinking about the situation. I'll be at work, filling drink orders, and I'll have a conversation with the shift supervisor about the mocha we have in stock or the retail we need to order, or a movie coming out next weekend. And for a moment, I answer her or I respond to her, or I even laugh with her. And the second that moment is over, I think to myself, *"What are you doing? Abbie's lost out there and counting on you! You're standing here at work, laughing. Why didn't you quit weeks ago? Isn't she more important than your paycheck?"*

I remind myself that keeping up the air of normalcy is going to help Abbie in the long run. If I dwell on things, it's not helping Abbie. I try desperately not to be obvious about my knowledge. Until I know more, I have to act like I know nothing.

When I get home from the show, in my room and pick up a picture of Abbie and me at Pismo Beach from last summer. Now it is a picture of Traveler and me. Now, I suppose, it was Traveler who sunbathed with me on the beach that day. It was Traveler who sat with me when we flirted with the surfers a few feet away. It was Traveler who fell asleep, leaning on my shoulder on the long drive home that night, sunburned and smelling like salt water.

I've consulted as many oracles as I can. Runes and cards both tell me that there is a powerful female influence exerting itself on the situation. No shit. Both runes and cards tell me that there is something going on monumental and mysterious. No, really?

Both runes and cards tell me that now is *not* the time for action. They both tell me that it is time to gather my wits and be patient, waiting for the ripeness of the moment. This is so hard to do. But something in my bones tells me it's true.

Tonight, though, is Imbolc. It is a time of magic and awakening. It is a good time to scry, and high time I did so. I've been putting it off, fearing the literal images that come across to me, fearing their news.

The first thing I do is prepare for the ceremony by bathing. I bath in salt water, made from sea salt. I don't think my landlord will be pleased with the way the salt water is treating the tub, but I'm not concerned at the moment. It is very important for me to bathe myself and cleanse my body and soul before ceremonies of great importance.

I pull my rug away from the floor and shove it under my bed, revealing the pentagram I have painted on the hardwood. I sprinkle the first buds and petals of spring around the edge of the pentagram. I picked them earlier from the garden in front of the Catholic Church near the mission. I get candles and incense out of the top drawer of my dresser—white candles, and incense that Abbie made for me. I suppose now, the incense was made by Traveler. I get my dagger, wrapped in silk, I get my wand, made of a birch branch, also wrapped in silk.

I place the candles around the pentagram. I set

the wand and the dagger on a small stool next to the pentagram. I go to the closet and get my cauldron. I fill it with full moon water. I set the cauldron at the top of my pentagram. I light the candles, light the incense, and step inside the pentagram.

In my left hand, I hold the dagger. In my right hand, I hold the wand. With the dagger, I draw my circle saying, "This is a circle of protection. Within this ring, symbolizing the eternal cycle of nature, I am protected by the Goddess, and by the Great Horned God, and I am defended by Their magic." I say these words carefully, but with meaning. I feel the power and confidence of lent immortality. I am free from harm within my circle, I become a holy vessel during the ceremony.

Then, I draw the circle again, this time with my wand. "Knowledge is welcome within this circle. I ask to be enlightened by the wisdom of those beings greater than myself. I offer myself to the knowledge and wisdom of the universe, both known and unseen, and will use this knowledge only for the good of the world."

I meditate on these words for a while. I can feel the knowledge breathed into me, like an icy wind, filling my body. When I am in my circle, I am transformed. I am not Erica, the witch-barista living in Ashlan, I am a human embodiment of The Goddess. I am bride to The Great Horned God—Father Nature.

I kneel in the dark candle light and before my cauldron. The water glistens and reflects the candle light. It reflects a changing web pattern on the ceiling that makes me think of the magical web of life, the way energy is interconnected between all living things. If all living things are one, then the benefit of one is the benefit of all. Harm to one is harm to all; thus the creed of my coven, "Harm none."

I gaze into the water, and meditate on the surface. I focus my eyes as if looking through the cauldron and into the ever changing future. I ask the cauldron to show me the path, show me the way that I can help Abigail. Show me the way that I can make things right again.

I stay kneeling for a matter of minutes, looking into the shapes. Then I see, as clear as day, an image of me walking up a mountain. I am walking up to a group of people on the crest of a hill, about half way up a mountain. Many of them are from my coven, but one is not. She is a girl of about 15 or 16 with dark auburn hair. She is stoic, straight faced, but has a third eye on her forehead. I hear the words of my grandmother coming back to me from when I was 13 years old, "up the mountain, my child. You will find enlightenment up the mountain." I turn to face the voice, as it is coming from behind me, and I see a small sparrow sitting on the window sill. The sparrow looks like my grandmother. I start to cry.

The spell, suddenly, is broken. The bird is gone, the cauldron is full of water, and the candles burn very, very low.

I stand in my circle and tell the gods that the circle is broken. I thank them for their wisdom. I thank them for their generosity. I thank them for their love, and for the life that they breathe into my form every morning.

Twenty-Seven

Abigail never understood why my family was in a coven. From what I understand, we weren't always, but there has always been a camaraderie of knowledge, coven or otherwise, in our family's history. Before my family joined the coven, we practiced with my grandparents at their home near Losa Valley, about half way up to Yosemite. My grandfather was a very wise man. He was raised in an orphanage in Kentucky, and found his religion through a fellow soldier in the Korean War. He married my grandmother, who was many years younger than him when he got back from that war. She was a full blooded Losa Indian, and her grandfather had been a medicine man in their tribe. She had been given a small chunk of almost unusable land by the government, and they lived there together all alone.

My grandmother accepted Wicca as a white interpretation of her religion. She still kept many of the names and practices of her beliefs when she practiced the Craft with us. She said that theirs was a happy marriage of two wonderful spirits, joined by the same spirituality.

When I was very young, my grandmother knitted me a star blanket. It was an enormous quilt, covered in the night's sky, as it looked the night that I was born. She explained to me that this blanket *was* me. It was not to be misinterpreted as anything else. She told me that the night covered me looking like this when life was first breathed into me, and that any time I needed protection, I needed to only cover myself with the same stars that gave me my awareness.

It was a beautiful blanket that my Mom rarely let me see. It was wrapped up and put in a box in my mom's closet. The box was made of wood and decorated by my grandfather to keep the blanket safe.

But on my 13th birthday, my grandmother decided that I should go on a vision quest. My older brother hadn't even gone on one yet; she said he wasn't ready. My mother was worried about me, but tried not to show it. I heard her at night talking to my grandmother, saying I was too young for something so serious. But my grandmother insisted, and Mom and Dad relented at last.

My parents dropped me off at my grandparents' house and headed back to town. Along with me, they left the box that contained my star blanket. It was early in the morning, but my grandmother said that we were in a hurry and must leave immediately.

My grandmother led me through a path in the forest and up a hill. I kept asking her where we were going, and all she would answer was, "Up the mountain, my child. You will find enlightenment up the mountain." We walked for hours and hours, only stopping once for a rest and to drink water. My feet were sore and forming blisters in my new shoes. I was astonished at my grandmother's ability to keep pressing on. She was never winded and only suggested the break because I had fallen a hundred yards behind her.

During the last hour of the walk, my grandmother told me not to talk at all. We were to be as quiet as possible, so as not to attract the attention of anything in the forest.

This comment frightened me beyond belief. I didn't know what it was that could be in the forest that she didn't want to attract.

We walked in silence the last hour. I had left my watch back at their house, as instructed, but I could tell that it was getting late. I wasn't sure how we were going to make it back by nightfall. Then, I imagined, that perhaps my grandmother and I were going to be spending the night up here. Why else would she be taking along that heavy canvas bag, I wondered.

Finally, we got to the peak of a very large hill, overlooking several valleys from any side. My grandmother beckoned me forward and showed me a pit that had been dug in the soft ground. It was about six feet in diameter, and maybe three feet deep.

"Here," my grandmother said quietly, only a little louder than in a whisper, "is where you will spend the next three days."

I was no longer only frightened, but outraged. Why did I have to do this? There were, no doubt, all kinds of bugs and animals that would harass me in that pit.

"My child," my grandmother said to me. "You will draw your circle here. You will be safe from everything in this pit. The first thing you will do is draw your circle."

"Grandmother," I said. "You can't leave me here. I don't want to be here."

"This is something you must go through alone," she said in a consoling tone. "We all must go through this alone. You will not be frightened." She sat down on the ground and opened up the bag she had been carrying with her. "You will stay up here three days. You will not eat or drink for three days."

"Grandma, that's impossible."

"Child," she said sternly. "This is very serious. You will not question what I have to tell you here. You will follow my directions to the last, do you understand?"

"Yes, Grandmother," I said.

She sat down in the pit and piled together some wood. On top of the wood, she placed an iron cauldron. "This cauldron is yours from now on," she said. "It will help to guide you." She poured water into the cauldron and then emptied a small sack into the water, of something that I couldn't recognize. "This is made from the red birch tree and the bark of a giant sequoia. When night falls, you will light this fire and get the pot to boiling. You will do whatever you can to make the pot boil all night long." She piled some wood on the far end of the pit.

"You will wrap your blanket around you," she unrolled my star blanket from her bag. "You will use it as a hood to catch the steam of the cauldron. You will not, no matter what, drink the water in this cauldron. You will surely die if you do. Now, sit down in the pit and wait for the Spirit to come to you. Now please, give me your clothes."

"My clothes?"

"You must perform this ceremony without them. You will wear the stars of this night and the stars from the night you were born. That is all."

I disrobed and handed my clothes over to my grandmother, who balled them up and put them in her canvas bag. "You have everything you need here, my child. I will be here in the morning three days from now. When you walk down the mountain, you will be a woman."

She turned around and walked away from me. I couldn't help but think that this must be some kind of a joke. I thought that at any moment during the night, I would have my entire family spring forth from the woods and sit with me under the stars.

I drew my circle anyway and waited for the surprise. This suspicion left me as I sat in the gathering darkness, and was able to see the small black dot of my grandmother between the trees far down the mountain. I lit the fire as I was told, and the resulting brew was very unpleasing to smell, and burned in my lungs. I held my blanket over me like a rooftop, letting the steam hover around my face.

What my grandmother said was true, I wasn't scared anymore. I felt protected and calm, naked in my blanket. Eventually, I felt like I was going to fall asleep. Instead, the fire stopped burning and I panicked to get it to live again. The sticks turned into bugs in my hands, huge nasty bugs with hundreds of legs. I screamed for someone to help me and I begged the Goddess and the Spirit to save me from these creatures.

A flock of small birds flew to me in the dark and began to peck at me, devouring the bugs off of my skin. When they were finished, I thanked them profusely. I told them that I was theirs to do what they would with, I was their servant from that moment on. The bird at the head of the flock perched on the rim of the cauldron.

"You have already pledged yourself to the Spirit. Do you rescind your pledge to the Spirit and to the Earth Mother Goddess?"

The bird's voice was powerful and feminine. "I do not rescind any such offering of myself."

"Then how do you propose to be the servant of us all?"

"Great bird," I said. "Are you not the Spirit? Are you not the child of the Earth Mother? Are we not all the same?"

The bird turned its head and smiled as much as a bird could. "You have pleased us tonight," it said. "The magical web of awareness is at your disposal. You may travel where you will and learn what you wish to know."

I was absorbed into my star blanket. I was soaked in like water, and found myself surrounded by stitched starlight. I was in flight as one of the small birds, seeing the world from their eyes. Through their eyes, I watched ages of lifetimes pass, seeing the women that went before me in my family line and what each of them did to pass on their knowledge and magic to their daughters. I saw their husbands, too, and felt their kindness and understanding, saw their wisdom and their longing.

The feeling was one of atonement. I was not alone on the mountain, but felt instead like I was a lifetime of women in one body. Every stitch my ancestors made in the quilt of knowledge was in me. From candle to candle, they passed their fire on. They were not historical figures, they were not distant relatives, they were living and connected and in me. I was possessed with the burning purpose to make that knowledge grow within me. I was consumed with the desire to add stitches of my own through my craft, and to pass it on when the time came.

At last, I was again sitting in the pit on the mountain top. In front of me was the cauldron resting on a pile of smoking leaves and twigs. On its edge was the little bird.

"Father Spirit," I said to the bird. "Am I not to receive a name for my practices? A magical name?"

The bird looked at me stoically. "Your name is your name. Don't argue with it. Your name is Erica. Your parents named you true. That is the only name you will ever have." The bird blinked and flew away.

The sun was rising behind me. I sat and watched as the sunlight painted the landscape in front of me, inch by inch. Then I heard footsteps coming up the hill, and it was my grandmother.

"We have a long way to walk," she said. She threw me the canvas bag that she had brought up with me. Inside it were my clothes. "We will walk down from the peak, and I will make you something to eat. Then we will walk home in silence. When we get there, you may tell me what happened to you on this mountain. But there is no need to, if you don't want to."

I dressed, and the idea of being clothed seemed foreign to me. We walked down the mountain, and I carried my cauldron and star blanket. They have been mine ever since.

THE TRAVELER

Twenty-Eight

I arranged a meeting with the High Priestess of our coven to speak about Abigail and her plight. She is a remarkable woman in her young 40's who has been High Priestess of this coven since she was 30 or so, before my family joined. She is strikingly beautiful and has long blond hair that curls and waves down her back. She always wears dresses and carries herself with a wonderful grace.

She looks just a little like she's ready for a Renaissance Fair to break out at any time.

"Your Lady," I say. We are meeting in her backyard. She lives outside of town and has a good deal of land that adjoins a river. The sun is out and the weather is getting warmer; winter doesn't last long in Ashlan.

"I have reached a very difficult path," I say. "I'm not even sure if I can explain what's happening in my life. And I know that it isn't believable."

"Why Erica," she says. "You know I'd believe anything you say."

This is where I tell her the story. This is where the details get fuzzy because everything is so strange and un-relatable. Her facial expressions show me that she is following the story, and as near as I can tell, she takes me very seriously.

"Tell me, Erica," she says at the close of my story. "Is your friend Abbie possessed, as far as you can tell?"

"No. It's not that. It's not a possession," I say. "Traveler *looks* like a different person. And everyone calls her Traveler. They remember her as always being there."

"This is a condition, I'm sure, that you escaped by witnessing the magical act that made this happen. You have no idea how fortunate that is, Erica. The chances of having your first successful regression coincide with this cataclysmic act are zero. The Goddess guided you to your friend's side that night. It seems as if the Goddess has chosen you to save the girl."

"How, Your Lady?"

"I don't know, exactly. I wish I did. I believe that the oracles are right; this is not the time to act, but a time to gather information. The obvious solution would be for Abbie and Traveler to undergo the same ceremony. But, I assume that Traveler will not be a willing participant."

"No, she won't."

"And yet," says the Priestess, in deep thought. "Your friend Abbie says that the world and her memories of it are slipping away from her. Is there any way to know if the same thing is happening to Traveler and her memories of the world before?"

"She doesn't know that I know. If she remembers

195

anything, she'll never speak about it to anyone."

"Not even Abbie?"

"Abbie has been unable to communicate with her so far. But even so, even if Traveler did forget her past existence, where would that put us? I don't see how that knowledge would help," I say.

"Maybe she can be tricked into trading places again, if she thinks that Abigail is nothing but an imaginary friend, just like Abbie thought of Traveler."

"But that could take years."

"There is a way to tell."

"We can't sit around and —"

"Hush, now," the Priestess says, holding her hand to stop me. "There is a way to tell. There is someone who can help. This man is no witch. He is a seer. I've met him on a few occasions, and he is amazing at what he does. Perhaps with his sight, we can determine how long it will be before Traveler loses her memory of her past, if ever."

"And if it's soon?"

"Then we can act sooner. We can find some way to get her to fall into the same trap that Abigail did. Some way to get her to do that same spell."

"And if it's never?" I ask.

"This man can tell us if there's any hope at all, actually," says the Priestess. "He is that good, if he is willing. We will know her outcome after talking to him. Or we will know what he chooses to share, at any rate. This man is flawless. I will contact him for you, but you will have to go see him yourself."

"Why don't you talk to him about everything?

Why isn't he here with us now?"

"Even with his ability, you can't take a shortcut through your human experience. I only consult him when it sounds like someone is at risk of *losing* their human experience."

"Where does he live?"

"Where do you think? In the mountains."

Twenty-Nine

The Priestess contacted the man for me, and he agreed to help me. She gave me directions to where he lived, and told me what day to go. She directed me right up highway 180, right passed my family's land. The land where I had my vision quest. The land where Abigail and I celebrated the Solstice.

Or was that Traveler, now? I was glad to be spared the memory.

Maybe, I kept thinknig, this man can help us break this spell.

All the same, I wasn't sure that this was a simple spell. When you talk to Traveler, you don't sense enchantment playing a role with her at all. You don't feel like your speaking to someone spell bound. There could be nothing more real than her. She is as solid and real as Abbie was when she was alive.

The night before driving up to the mountains, I flew over to Abigail's room to try and tell her what was being done about the situation. Things were grim there, as I feared. I hadn't visited for a while, for dread of seeing Abigail's situation as it stands now. I've felt really bad about it, but a visit with her can get me down for days on end, even though it means so much to her.

"I spoke with my Priestess, Abbie," I said. "We think there may be a way to get you back. We're trying to work on it now, and we'll need your help later on."

Abigail was sitting in her bed hugging her knees against her chest. As usual, her eyes were locked on me, burning a hole right through my little bird body.

"Really, Erica, don't worry about it. There's no reason fussing over me anymore. I'm not fussy over it. You shouldn't be, either. Things are fine."

"Abigail, you have to snap out of it. You have to keep remembering your life. You have to keep remembering how important you are to everyone. It's not Traveler's right to have your life."

Abigail spoke very softly. "Erica, I don't deserve the life any more than she does. You say I mean something to you? Do you want to know what I did?"

"I don't want to hear it, Abbie."

"Too bad. This is part of me remembering my life. This is part of it, so just listen. I tried to banish you during my Samhain ritual."

"What?"

"I picked a word for you, *Fear*. I was frightened of you, of what you meant in my life. I had finally decided that I would cut you out of it."

"Abbie, this is the depression talking."

"No, it is not. It's perfectly true. I didn't trust you. Not fully. And I was afraid of how I felt towards you. And here you are now, doing everything you can, dropping everything in your life to try and save me."

"It's nothing, Abbie, really. It's my duty as a—"

"It's your duty nothing," she said. "Erica, did you cast a binding spell on me?"

"A what? A binding spell?" I was outraged at the accusation. "Why in the world would I do that?"

"To keep me from taking Vic from you."

"For Christ's sake, Abbie, I told you a thousand times that I didn't want Vic. How many times did I tell you that?"

"See what I mean, Erica?" Abbie is again totally non-emotional. "I don't deserve your help. I don't deserve you. I actually believed Traveler when she told me you had a binding spell on me."

"Abbie," I said calmly, "I've always wanted *you*."

"Did you cast a love spell on me?"

"Oh my gods!" I yelled. "In my coven, a love spell is considered *black* magic. We never touch black magic. Ever. Not under any circumstance. Where did you get that idea?"

"See? I don't deserve you. Traveler told me that you put a love spell on me and I believed her. And I followed her directions when she told me to put a love spell on Vic."

"You put a *love spell* on Vic?"

"I did," Abbie said, sadly. "I did. And it worked, for the most part, to get him to at least be real around me."

"Why?"

"Erica, don't waste your energy on me. Don't waste your time. Make friends with Traveler. You said yourself she's a very amiable girl. She'll make a good friend to you. I've been a very bad one."

I felt like crying. I hated to see Abigail acting like this. "Abbie, don't talk to me this way. You've been a wonderful friend. It's no trouble for me to help you. You need to come back."

"How long has it been, Erica? I'm sure it's not worth it anymore."

"It's hasn't been that long. Just a few weeks."

"It feels like years."

"I'm sorry I'm not with you more," I said. "I'll try to be here more often. But if this lead pays off, then you won't be here much longer. Or at least we will know how much longer."

"You say you're going to need my help?"

"Yes, Abbie."

"I won't help. I think I should stay here. I think you should move on. I love you, Erica. Goodbye. This has to be goodbye."

"Don't let me leave on this note, Abbie," I said, frustrated. "I'm doing everything I can for *you*. I don't want to let you go away like this."

"We'll see, Erica," she said. "I'm so hungry. I'm so tired. I can't eat. I can't sleep. All I can do is sit here and count my hands when you're gone."

"How many times have I been here? Do you remember?"

"How should I know? I have no idea. I don't know how often you come or anything, because when you're not here or Traveler's not in the room, I don't have any idea that I exist at all. It's miserable, Erica, really it is."

It was the most disheartening visit I've had with her. And as I busy myself with trying to help her, or as I busy myself with real life, I'm comforted by the fact that she doesn't know how long I'm gone from her. I wish I could be there more, but if I leave for five minutes or if I leave for a week, she has no idea what the difference is.

I know that our plan, so much as it stands right now, is dependent on Traveler forgetting her former life. But it's looking more and more like Abigail is going to lose her mind before that happens.

I drive my truck up the mountains, past my family's land. The trees get taller and taller, and soon I'm up high and off in the distance I can see Ashlan. I turn down a road off of the highway and travel another three miles. Then I turn right where I see a gate that is open. I end up pulling into the driveway of a very big house - a mansion really, three stories high, with pillars going up the height of it. I remember hearing the Priestess say that this man wasn't a witch, and now I know why she pointed that out to me; no witch that I've ever met would have a house so conspicuous, even in such a remote place.

I park the car and walk up to the door. I ring the bell, but don't hear anything. A few moments later, the door is answered by a very tall, very large man in his sixties or so.

"Hello," I say. "Are you Red?"

"I am," he says. "We've been expecting you.

Come in, please."

I am led into a very large and open room. The back wall of the room is all window, two stories high, and looks into a forest. The room is stunning, I've never seen anything like it. The centerpiece of the room is a very ornate grand piano.

"Wow," I can't help but say.

Red sits down on a sofa and motions for me to sit on the one across from it. "So," he says. "Sounds like your friend went and let the genie out of the bottle."

"I suppose so, sir. You can help us?"

"I'm afraid not," he says.

"But the Priestess said—"

"Don't worry, she didn't mislead you," he says. "I have someone who will help. But we have to discuss the nature of the arrangement."

"What arrangement?"

"You don't think that I got this house by doing favors, do you? We usually exact quite a price. But since Nadine is an old friend and has helped me out quite a bit, I've agreed to make special arrangements."

The nature of this talk is a little disturbing. I have gone from feeling very comfortable to feeling like I stepped into the spider's web.

"I figured you just guessed a few lottery numbers, sir. What could I possibly have that you'd want?"

He smiles. "Listen. My daughter," Red says, "will be helping you. She will be of much more help than I could be, anyway. She's not just a seer, she's a feeler as well."

"Excuse me sir," I say. "Can you please tell me exactly what a seer *is*? And how do you propose to help my friend?"

"Isn't it obvious? A seer can foresee the events of the future."

I am taken aback by how calmly he puts this across, as if I should be no more surprised than if he had just told me that a painter paints.

"A feeler has a different ability," he continues. "A feeler can sense a person's emotional past. And from that make up, she can effectively tell you about the subject's whole history."

"Really?"

"Well, a good one can. And I assure you that Tydomin is becoming a very good one."

Just as he finishes saying this, a girl enters the room. She is a teenager, maybe 15 or 16, and is clearly the girl I saw in my scrying. She has no third eye, but I had already begun to accept the idea that the third eye had to have been some kind of metaphor given to me by the gods.

"Hello," she says, looking at me. She is carrying a suitcase in each arm. "Are we just about ready to go?"

Confused, I turn and look at Red.

"Tydomin is moving to Ashlan," he explains. "And she will be staying with you for a few months, just until she can find her own place and job."

I am speechless. "I don't have a lot of room, sir. And no money."

"I can pay for myself," the girl says. "I just need

someone to show me around. I need to get used to things."

"What, I'm supposed to tutor you through grade school? Did the Priestess know about this?"

"Nadine suggested it. We had a long conversation, and she knew that you would help us out. And don't worry, she is finished with her schooling."

I feel very on the spot. "I don't know if I have the room, honestly, it's very small place. I need a few days to work out the logistics of it."

Red looks at me impatiently. I can feel his disapproval weighing heavily on me. I just have to find a way to get out of here. I wish I hadn't come. I don't know what a psychic is going to do to help the situation, anyway.

"Erica," Tydomin says. She puts her bags down and walks over to the couch where I am sitting. She sits next to me and reaches out for my hands, which I give to her, out of politeness. "I know that you're hesitant to open up your home to me. And I understand that. But it is very important that you do so, if you want to help Abigail out. I want you to think about the time that you met Abigail. You picked her up from her parents' house, and she was like a lost and lonely child to you. You felt pity that her mother had died, and you tried to avoid talking about it.

"But then, finally, on the way home, you talked about her mom. You talked about her openly, you felt better. You weren't blocked or hindered by anything in talking to her anymore. Do you remember that?"

"Of course I do," I say.

"Abigail was relieved by that moment, too. It was the first time that someone that had known her mom talked to Abigail like she was a person, and not an object of pity. You let go of your pity and you saw Abbie for what she is. And it paid off for you. You got a friend in that moment."

"Is this supposed to amaze me, or endear me, Tydomin?" I ask.

"You miss Abbie, don't you?"

"Of course I do. Anyone would know that."

"I know that you've spoken to her since she's stopped existing. I can tell you a lot about this Traveler. I can tell you where she comes from. I can tell you what she is, I think. With that kind of information, you'll at least know what you're fighting. But best of all, I can tell you when to strike her."

"God, you make it sound so aggressive."

"Erica," Red interrupts. "If you think this is going to be a game, you're wrong. Aggression is surely something that is going to come into play."

"That's another thing," I say. "Why is it that you two believe me?"

They don't react to this comment but just look at each other.

"You don't trust us because we believe you?" Red asks. "That doesn't make much sense."

"I didn't believe you," Tydomin says. "Not until I walked out here and met you. Your emotions are very connected to this girl. *Very* connected." The way she looks at me, I know what she's referring to. She sees me kissing her, and she can feel how I feel about her. And she's not bringing it up so that I'm not embarrassed in front of her father. "I'm not the seer that my dad is," she continues. "But with time, I can see how this is going to play out. I need to be around you, to be around Traveler, I need to see everything. We need each other, I promise you."

There is a long moment of silence where I sit and contemplate all of this. This silence is taken for agreement, and I never call their bluff. Red takes Tydomin's bags out to the car, then comes back in and says, "I'll get the rest of your things now, too." He makes himself busy while I sit on the sofa next to Tydomin, who isn't smiling or frowning.

"Are you always so serious?" I ask her.

"What do you mean?"

"You seem pretty, you know, stoic. Why are you moving away from here anyway? You have any idea what my apartment looks like? The whole thing could fit inside that piano."

"I know what your apartment looks like," she says. "I drew a picture of it a couple of months ago. You're not too worried about getting your security deposit back."

"No, but that doesn't mean that you can make a mess of things."

And here she smiles.

Thirty

I am driving down the mountain with my new roommate. I've never lived with someone before, and I dread the idea of it. Not to mention she's a child of 16 that I've never met before, and she's already planning on junking up my apartment.

Red filled the bed of my truck with paintings that Tydomin has made and her art supplies. Tydomin is a wonderful painter, I can tell just by glancing at her work. She must be bringing two or three dozen canvasses of different sizes that you would never guess were painted by someone of her age.

"Where did you learn to paint?" I ask her.

"In my room," she says seriously.

"No one taught you."

"Oh, no. It's been very therapeutic for me. I've had a very hard time growing up, and the painting has helped me to organize my experiences. It helped me make my implicit experiences explicit, so I understand it all more clearly."

I can tell that Tydomin didn't get out of her gilded cage much when she was growing up. "What do you mean by that, Tydomin?"

"It took me a long time to separate things in my head," she says. "I was born being able to see the future and feel the past. It was almost impossible for me to locate myself in the present with all of that going on. But, that didn't stop me from making implicit memories that I used to navigate the world, see? Red and I have never heard of anyone else born like me. We suspect it's happened, but we also suspect they lost their minds at a young age."

"You call him Red?"

"I do," she says. "You know, I never see him again."

"Who?"

"Red. That was the last time I ever see him."

I remember back to when we left she told him goodbye and he told her goodbye, but they didn't hug or exchange other words. It was the kind of farewell you might give your dad when he is on his way to work, not when you're never going to see him again.

"Did you know that when you left?"

"Oh, yes. That's why I had to leave. He dies before very long. He has a lot to get in order for his death, and I don't want to get in the way. I have to learn to have my own life away from him."

"Of course," I say. "Aren't you sad?"

"That's something that I'm still trying to work on. I have a hard time regretting that he is going to die. On one level, it's kind of my fault. I changed something that I saw and it leads to this all (long story). But on another level, it's emotionally impossible for me to access the situation. But when he does, I'm sure I'll be very, very broken up about it. I feel like if I could take off some of the emotional strain now, I wouldn't react is such a bad way when I do hear about it. But so far, I have never been able to get emotional about an event in the future. I think it might be impossible."

"You're never going to talk to him again?" I ask.

"We will mail each other, but that is all."

"You said you caused it all. Is there any way to *stop* him from dying?"

Tydomin is quiet for a while, looking out the window. "We trust our decisions, Erica. I see now that we just *have* to."

"What do you mean?"

"Our future is based on our decisions. We trust them. We trust that we make all of our decisions for the right reasons. If we start to meddle with our decisions, we lose our integrity. And then things start to fall apart."

"Which is more important? Your integrity or your life?"

"Exactly," Tydomin says. "You get it."

She is a pretty girl, this Tydomin. But I am unnerved being near her.

Thirty-One

We get Tydomin moved in to my apartment alright. She says that she doesn't mind sleeping in her sleeping bag on the floor. I feel terrible about this because I know that she must be leaving some kind of amazing goose-down-whatever-fancy-bed behind at her father's house. She piles her paintings in my closet, and is constantly apologizing for how much space she's taking up. She's also very interested in my Wicca equipment, but she doesn't ask me about any of it, she just looks and wonders. Somehow I don't think a lot of talking was in her upbringing.

She insists on seeing Traveler that night if possible, so we can get started on the project. I have to say that even though I'm not totally comfortable with this arrangement, I am very happy to be taken seriously. Abbie has been gone for over four months now, and I've been dying to talk about it with someone. Now that I hear myself discussing it, I can't help but to start doubting the whole thing. Talking about it is like taking something from the dark and moving it to the light. It seems like an illusion in the light of day.

It is the first time I've been to the Andante on a Sunday night since Abbie disappeared. It's so strange to me that Traveler has adopted so many aspects of Abbie's life. I'm not sure if it's because she was just so jealous of Abbie, or if it has something to do with the manner in which Traveler took her life. Does she have to step in to all of her roles, or does she choose to?

Or, wow, did she help give her those roles in the first place?

The Andante is packed. Absolutely full. Vic told me that the place gets crowded now, and I remember seeing that conversation as a way to try and jar him into remembering Abigail. Abbie told me not to worry about that; that probably we were in some kind of parallel world now, a pocket universe or whatever, where it has always been that way. But I can't help to but to think that if we crossed over, so can he.

"You should see the place these days," Vic said to me. "It's insane how many people they can load into there on a Sunday."

"What do you think changed?" I asked him.

"What do you mean?"

"Why is it so packed all of a sudden? We used to go watch her play and there would hardly be anyone there. What do you think the difference is now?"

Vic thought about it for a while. "I'm not sure. Word got out, I suppose, about how good she is."

"Do you remember the night last November when you and I sat at a table together? She was playing a Joni Mitchell song, and you told me about when the two of you…you know?"

"Yeah."

"Do you remember all the turmoil you were going through? How you hated the fact that you hurt her feelings and you wanted to ask me for advice on how to help? You remember all that."

"Of course I do, Erica."

"Look how different things turned out. Don't you think?"

"You never know, I guess."

"No," I said. "You never know."

It was one of the many frustrating conversations I've had in the past few months, where I just want to scream out, *"What the fuck is wrong with you? Don't you remember Abbie? Your friend? Don't you remember the girl who you fucking grew up with? Snap the hell out of it!"* But I don't. The last thing I want in this whole world is for Traveler to know that I know her secret. It's so damn hard.

Vic is sitting at a table, and although it's a scramble, I'm able to flirt a couple of chairs away from some guys so Tydomin and I can sit with him. I introduce Tydomin as an old family friend, and it seems to go over well enough. I order myself a cappuccino and Tydomin orders water. Great social skills, right?

"This is some crowd," I say to Vic. "Has she started playing yet?"

"She's just tuning up right now," Vic says.

"I just can't get over how popular this is. Does she sing the same set that she used to?"

"It's not really a set that she sings," Vic says. "Not anymore. I can't believe you haven't come in so long. What kind of friend are you?" he jokes.

"Oh, I don't know, Vic, a busy one?"

"That must be it."

When Traveler greets the crowd, a lull comes over the hundred or so people packed in to the small café. I look over at Tydomin and motion with my chin towards Traveler, signifying that this is our girl.

"Hello everyone," Traveler says meekly into her microphone. "I'd just like to tell all of you how much it means to me that you come out here and spend your Sunday nights with me. I don't know what I ever did without all of you."

The audience applauds politely, touched by the sincerity of Traveler's voice.

"As usual, we're going to start off pretty quietly here. So thank you for your patience with me, for your respected silence, and thank you for coming. Please lower the lights."

The lights in the café shut down to a bare minimum. Traveler brings her cello against her body and into playing position. Before even drawing the bow across the string, her left hand rolls vigorously against the finger board for the vibrato. Her eyes close and her face somewhat contorts as if she were feeling our collective pain.

"Oh, come on," I say under my breath. "Get on with it and stop with the dramatics already." The audience sits on the edge of the seats. My eyes roll.

Slowly, Traveler draws the bow across the string.

At first you can't hear anything, but then I realize that she is pulling out the sweetest note I've ever heard played on the cello. Her bow seems to go on forever as the low note fades to the tip of the bow. Her hand changes direction and she pushes out a note higher; that note then slides up to the high portion of the finger board, and the spirits of the entire audience are jerked up higher. The feeling is genuinely ecstatic, even for me.

As she continues with the slowly droning cello, she begins to sing. Her singing soars over the voice of the cello. Her eyes are still closed as she calls out a slow, alto harmony to the tenor of the cello.

Tears are in my eyes, literally. I look over at Vic, who is absorbed and I cannot get him to look at me. I look at Tydomin and her eyes and mouth are all spread wide. There's an enchantment to this music that goes far beyond what we're hearing. We are pulled on and lifted up, moved and dropped, all by the lines of melody and harmony of this girl and her cello. I can't tell if this is the greatest music I've ever hear, or if this is pure magic; a powerful spell cast over all the listeners.

The song gets louder and faster. Her words are from some language that I am totally unfamiliar with, or they're just purely music phonetics that couldn't be more perfect if they communicated anything literary. The song becomes chant-like, as the words - or what's passing for words - get more rhythmic and play counterpoint with the cello. We, the audience, move in the waves of the music.

The audience breathes as one. We breathe along with her cadence, with her rhythm, with her dipping, waving melodies. No one moves or talks on their own. The counter isn't selling drinks. The cashier is listening, leaning on her hands, with her eyes shut tightly. While I am moved and touched and amazed by what I hear, I seem to be the only one not *completely* immobilized by her song. I am the only one who seems capable of looking around and letting my attention waver from just the docile sitting and listening. I don't *want* to not pay attention, but I am too fascinated with everyone's reaction to let myself get lost entirely in her music. Still, I find myself lost within individual moments, wishing I had come sooner, wishing I could hear this song again.

The song lasts for 45 minutes without any kind of break. In the 45 minutes, I don't see one person leave, get up to go to the bathroom, ask for a refill, or so much as talk to the other people at their table. They're locked in ecstasy, with Traveler steering them any way she wants, her voice ringing like some beautiful instrument.

At the conclusion of the very strange concert, the crowd applauds wildly and thankfully. Traveler stands and bows, blushing with shy affection for her crowd. I clap, too, in earnest. I catch sight of Tydomin wiping her eyes as she claps.

The café bursts into motion and talk again and we are back in the real world. People stand and stretch, talk and drink. A good portion of the people walk outside and light their cigarettes. A light and joyful mood prevails over the café, with laughter and conversation. Tydomin looks at me excitedly, as if she never knew that moving away from home could ever be so engaging and wonderful.

"What did you think?" Traveler asks me when she comes to sit down, dripping with sweat. "This was your first time, right Erica?"

"I have to tell you, Traveler, I've never heard anything like it."

"Really? Did you like it?" Traveler seems to really want my approval.

"I can't explain how wonderful your music is, Traveler," I say sincerely.

"I'm so glad you liked it. I'm so glad that you came." Traveler is beaming with pride; a smile is pasted on her face.

"Traveler," Tydomin says, "I am awestruck. I've heard how wonderful your music is, but I have never been so touched by a performance in my life. And my father was a wonderful pianist. Your music is enchanting beyond words. Have you thought about taking this to a larger venue?"

Traveler is touched by this. I wonder how many times a night she has to hear a compliment to stop being so moved by them. It seems as if she will never reach her limit. "And you are?" she asks of the girl.

"My name is Tydomin, but you can call me Ty."

"Thank you, Ty."

"I am an old friend of Erica's. I'll be staying with her for a while."

"Oh," she says turning to me. "You never told me

about her."

"I didn't think she would interest you, Traveler," I say.

"I'm from out of state," Tydomin says.

Vic offers to buy us all a drink and we take him up on it. We sit there, the three girls and Vic, and talk about music for a while. Tydomin is active in the conversation. She seems to feel included and welcome ever since Traveler's performance. I am relieved by this because she's been so uptight and serious ever since I met her.

I'm getting very tired. It's been an extremely long day, and I still want to visit Abigail before I go to sleep tonight. But while my mind is made up, Tydomin seems willing to sit and talk to the demon forever.

Thirty-Two

"It's so good to see you," Abbie says when I arrive. "I don't remember if we've gone over this before, but you don't need to stay your power animal while traveling."

I am perched on the footboard of Abbie's bed, in the form of my regression, the finch. "I never really thought of that," I say.

"You've been reading, right? I mean, you don't need to be your animal to travel. I really used it for other things."

"I'm sorry, Abbie. It just feels so good. And I think it helps me stay in the dreaming state. How do I get out of it?"

"I don't remember," she says.

"Try, Abbie, try and tell me how to get out of this shape."

Abbie sits there and thinks. "Breathe," she finally says. "Breathe deep breaths, and with every one of them, try and imagine yourself becoming more like your human body. Breathe out the bird body."

I do this, and it works. I feel like Erica again, sitting on the bed.

"How many times have you been here and

stayed a bird?" Abbie asks me, a little amused.

"At least a couple dozen," I say. "It's so easy to travel, and it feels so good."

"I'm not offended," she says. "It's just so good to look at you again. To look at you like *you*." She stares at me for a while. "Your light is brighter this way, too. Did you cut your hair?"

"Yes," I say. "Do you like it?" I always have my hair long, but this cut is shorter and has felt very liberating.

"God," she says. "It's so sad that your life is just going on. You've gone and got your hair cut one day. That makes me so sad to think about."

I feel horribly about this. It's exactly the kind of thing I always feel bad about lately. I was dreadfully tired, but came out to see Abbie anyway out of guilt. It was late when we got home, after midnight, and I have no idea what time it is now. I have the opening shift at Starbucks in the morning, so there's no doubt I'll be getting no sleep at all tonight to speak of. Traveler isn't here, and that's what really matters.

I was here once when Traveler showed up, and even though I know that she can't perceive me while I'm here, I was so unnerved to see her that I was awake in my apartment too soon to really assess the situation.

Abbie sits there, looking forlorn, with the shadow of a smile on her face. Visiting Abbie these days is like visiting a terminal patient in a hospital; she sits there and speaks to you as if she's at peace with her eminent death.

The only difference with Abbie is that she acts as

if she's already dead.

"I picked up the girl that's supposed to help us," I tell her.

"What girl is that?"

"The girl from the mountains who can see the future."

"Ahh," says Abbie. "The seer's daughter. Did I tell you that my mom met the seer and told me about him a few times?"

"Yes, you did, Abbie."

"What's she like?"

"She's strange. We went and watched Traveler as she played your gig down at the Andante."

"How was that?"

I'm not sure what to say to this. I want to beam about Traveler's singing, but I don't want to seem like I'm going soft on her. If I tell Abbie that she is much better than her changeling, she will know I'm lying.

"She's a hell of a singer, isn't she?" Abbie says.

"Yes, Abbie. She is one hell of a singer."

"What did the girl find out about Traveler?"

I tell Abbie about our walk home from the café. I tell her about how we left late, some of the last people there on a Sunday night, and that the mile or so home, Tydomin and I discussed Traveler.

I leave out some details. I leave out how much Tydomin adored Traveler.

"Wasn't she wonderful?" she said to me, walking home. "I've never seen anything like her. She was mesmerizing. What an amazing creature."

"Wait, you mean that you couldn't see how much

you were going to like the show? This process confuses me."

"This is the kind of thing that I really need to work on," she tells me. "I couldn't look forward to the show or be excited about it, or know how much I was going to like it."

"Why not?"

"Because my love of her music was an emotional response. The future is void of emotion. I can see it all, and I can even see that I was going to be talkative about the whole thing. But I never could have known how heartbreaking and wonderful the music would be until it touched me. And when I look forward to something, it's probably a lot like how a regular person looks forward to something."

"A regular person?"

"You know, a typical-seeing person, like you," she says.

What I did tell Abbie was the things that Tydomin learned from looking at her with her special perceptions.

"The girl told me that Traveler is a very old creature. She's so old, she doesn't really remember what she is or where she comes from. But she was something else before."

"I suppose I don't remember being born," Abbie says. "But she must know *what* she is."

"She was a girl, about our age when she was changed."

"Changed into what?"

"As far as she can tell, Traveler was an apprentice

to a witch somewhere in Europe hundreds of years ago. She got into some trouble and ended up being absorbed into a tree as punishment. Some kind of a curse or a bleeding or something. It sounds grim. Ty says that her emotional baggage goes a few hundred years back. And that for a few more hundred years, she was trapped in this tree and then in this wood. Somehow she managed to stay in some form of existence in this bed."

"Is she some kind of spirit?"

"Yes, or an entity, or whatever we want to call it. Not fully human or fully tree, just a stray consciousness that is somehow born of all of it. She has been trying to get out for centuries."

Abigail looks up at me and says, "This doesn't tell us anything. What's the use?"

"She apparently adopted the identity from your mom, and started believing that she was her unborn daughter. Was this when she was pregnant with you, and your mom started talking to Traveler?"

"I mean, no? My mom didn't sleep in this bed when she and dad were married. It doesn't matter," Abbie said, as if the question were worth avoiding. "So she takes on this identity and believes it enough to tell me the same damn thing when I'm a little girl. But how does she get put back in the wood and how do I get out?"

"You're not going to like this," I say, mirroring the response that Tydomin gave me. "It's going to be a while before she's vulnerable. It's going to be next Halloween when you will have a chance to strike. And you're going to have to strike with a tool that she has locked in *your* world. She couldn't manage to bring it with her and she has it hidden somewhere."

I, of course, was very confused by this process again.

"Tydomin," I had said to her. "If you *knew* you were going to tell me that it was going to be next Halloween before she was vulnerable, why did you have to go as *see* her to tell me?"

Tydomin looked at me questioningly. "How else would I have found that out to tell you, if I didn't go to see her? I wouldn't have known that I was going to say it if I didn't."

Abigail listened with patience while I related the story. "It makes sense," she finally says. "Samhain is the best time to cross worlds. Traveler was powerful enough to pull me over whenever she wanted, but we're just normal witches. Samhain would be the best time. How close are we to it?"

I frown and consider lying to her. "It's not yet Beltane," I finally tell her.

Abbie's face falls a few feet lower. "Oh, Erica. I won't last that long. I just *can't* last that long. I'll be gone from whatever world this is by then."

Her response makes me want to cry. "No you won't!" I yell at her. "You're going to last, Abigail, do you hear me? I'm going to visit you and remind you about your life. You're going to keep following through with our plan, do you hear?"

"I hear you, Erica. I just don't know if I *want* to last till next Samhain."

I reach out and hug her. She feels cold to me, and the feeling frightens me. "How are things going with your project?"

"Same as always," she says. "She either can't hear me or she chooses not to. I feel pretty damn helpless."

"Remember the Solstice, Abbie?"

"Erica, if I disappear into this bed, I will always remember the Solstice," she says sweetly. "It was one of my fondest."

"Then you need to remember that you have to face the darkness of life with the faith that the sun will come back. Trust the Goddess. Trust the path. In the meantime, you have to try and find whatever it is that's hidden in your world. I don't know, a book, a wand - Ty couldn't really tell."

I can read in her eyes that she may not have the faith the light will come back this time. I don't blame her.

Thirty-Three

I watch as Erica flies out the window, again a small bird. I am amused at how she has such an affinity for turning into that little bird. It's probably the happiest thought that I have anymore, if it could be called a thought.

One of the exercises that I do regularly to try and keep my sanity is to repeat in my mind every word of my conversations with Erica after she leaves. Sometimes I'll do this three or four times, and sometimes I get distracted by the darkness before then. I sit and I recite, as best I can our conversation. I recite to myself what she learned from the seer's daughter, about Samhain being the time to strike. I remember that she said it wasn't yet Beltane, which left a good chunk of the year wasted for me. I remember what she said about the Solstice. And I get stuck thinking about that for a while.

In the middle of my recapitulation, the door of the room opens and Traveler comes in, leading Vic. Their light is beautiful to see, especially Vic's.

Traveler doesn't bring Vic here often, but I am always excited when she brings *anyone* into my room. I must feel like a prisoner would if the scenery outside his window changed just a little one day. Once, Traveler brought Erica back, and it was amazing to see Erica's living body, very different from her astral form, as far as my perception is. They sat and talked about Wicca, and Erica showed Traveler a type of tarot spread that Traveler didn't know. I didn't know it either, which made perfect sense, since Traveler seems to have assimilated all my knowledge pretty well.

Erica was aware of me the entire time she was there. I could tell because her aura was ill at ease. She was courteous and sweet to Traveler. I didn't get the impression that she was all that revolted by the imposter. Under different circumstances, I think the two of them cold have been very good friends.

"It's a good time to hit up some garage sales, Erica," Traveler said. "It's been an awful long time."

"It has been a while," Erica returned. "I could use another bed in my apartment. I have that roommate now."

"Why doesn't she get her own bed?"

"She refuses. I think she knows I'm going to crumble and get her one."

Suddenly Traveler laughed a full belly laugh. "I would never sleep on a mattress from a garage sale. God knows what's on that thing."

Erica laughed, too. "Me neither, but I told you that it wasn't for me." Then they both laughed.

"A twin mattress would fit in the bed of your truck easy," Traveler said.

"Oh, I know," Erica said. "I used to keep one

back there in the summer. I would drive up to my parents' land in the mountains and look at the stars in the bed. There's nothing like sleeping out under the stars. And on a mattress, it's wonderful."

"Ooo," Traveler cooed. "That sounds so nice. Maybe we could go up there when it gets warm enough."

And to this, Erica smiled. She's either a wonderful actress, or she is really starting to enjoy Traveler's company. I don't blame her if she does.

"We could use some time to reconnect," Traveler said. "I've felt a little distant from you lately."

It is painful for me to watch this, but I absolutely must. Watching their glow is so enchanting. And, gathering by the way Erica glowed when Traveler said this, she is somewhat excited.

"I'm afraid that maybe..." and here, Traveler acted very shy. "...I'm afraid that I came on a little strong, maybe."

"No, no, Traveler," Erica said. "Not at all. It was a beautiful moment between us. A beautiful moment that I will never forget." And here Traveler shyly looked at the ground, but Erica looked over to me, to the bed, with her eyes full of tears. "What happened on that mountain, for me, was one of the most wonderful moments I've ever had." Erica said this still looking at me. Then her voice changed tone and she looked back to Traveler and made eye contact with her. "But we can leave it at that. I think that it's best that we leave that behind us."

"Are you serious?" Traveler said, acting hurt. "I

think we should leave our options opened."

"I don't think so, Traveler," Erica says. "That moment was between me and the girl on the mountain. If that time ever comes back, conditions would have to be pretty identical."

From there, they rattled off again, talking about mundane things, everyday life. The type of things that tickle me and inspire me so much to hear these days.

One time, Dad was in here talking to Traveler. She asked him about his day, and he answered.

My dad gave her an honest and detailed answer about his day. He talked about how he'd had a department meeting first thing in the morning. He wasn't at all happy with the report from the Faculty Senate regarding the pay scale change, and how it was almost sure not to be approved by the administration. After the meeting, he'd held office hours. A student came in and gave him the absurd excuse that he was going to miss class due to a make-up test in a course that Dad knew wasn't offered that semester; Dad let it fly. He'd had a dental appointment in the afternoon and he hated having his teeth cleaned with that damn hook.

When I was alive, these kinds of answers bored me into a dormant state. I would have stopped listening before he finished the words "Faculty Senate," and would have retained nothing before it, out of sheer desire not to.

But now, I wanted to hear more. I wanted to ask what else was discussed in the meeting. What did the room look like? Who was there? Did people raise their hands to talk like school children in their meetings, or did everyone speak out when they had something to say? What was the course that the student said he needed to take the test for? Was it a good course? What sort of things can one learn in a course like that? What flavor toothpaste did they use to clean your teeth? Was it the bubble gum or the fruit flavor? *Dad,* I would have asked, *Do you like the way that dentist toothpaste is gritty when it's left in your mouth, or does it really bother you?*

From there we would have had wonderful discussions about everything one can think of. His meeting could have lead into conversations about government, higher education, public education, expectations of students, and so much more. The student's excuse could have led into discussions about lies that we've told and why we hid the truth, and how those truths would have affected the people we lied to. We would have talked about the fact that we lie to the people we love to protect them, or to keep their love. And I would have told him about three dozen lies I told him over the years and my reasons for doing it.

I realized in that moment how I had taken things for granted. I realized that from a simple day in a person's life, anything in all of creation can be talked about. There's a magical connectivity between everything we experience every day, and the experiences of every single other person on Earth. You walk out your door, and you've effectively done something to make a connection between yourself and all of humanity, past and present. It was a beautiful thing, life.

And how bored I had been with it. How boring I must have been. I think about Teri, all the times she tried to talk to me, and how I wished she would just leave. How I'd love to talk to her now.

But now I am watching Traveler and Vic play with the idea of getting physical. It's just so obvious what she's trying to do, and it's obvious he wants to fall for it, but he wants to be the one to start it. Ugh. I get the impression that Dad and Teri are somewhere out of town.

They strip each other's shirts off, and I am forced to sit and watch as their lights and their energies merge. I am forced to remember how this happened between Vic and me, and how I actually let something like that get me down, unable to cope with such a thing in my life. I was more of a child than I thought.

I can't tell what they have done or haven't done, as I get lost in my own mind, my own memories. But now I know that Dad is out of town because they turn out the light and fall asleep in each other's arms. It is time for me to start my nightly ritual of trying to wake Traveler so that we may have a word with each other.

I tried whispering in the beginning, now I try singing. I know that singing is what first alerted me to her presence, so every night I try singing to her, at least for a little while. I usually sing whatever comes to mind, and tonight, looking at Vic, I sing a song of his.

All she ever wanted, all she ever needs
Is for me to say I love her, and a drug to make it real.
It's a crime for me to sit here, and pretend she's in my

head

With my cold and twisted covert, what you think is what I say

Traveler doesn't budge, but Vic does. He looks at me, does what looks like a double-take, then he says, quietly, as if his mouth remembered the word before he did, "Abigail?"

I smile.

He looks confused.

"We have a so much to talk about, Vic."

The confusion on his face, I meet with a smile. I've been spending all my time trying to talk to Traveler, I never thought I could reach out to Vic. She must not have thought so, either, to bring him back. But his expression, while staying the same, seems to move over a landscape of epiphanies.

"I don't understand," he says, and he looks over at Traveler lying next to him. "What the hell is going on?"

"Do you remember me?" I try and keep a happy expression pasted to my face.

"I don't know. My memory is all mixed-up. This doesn't make any sense."

He sits up in bed and I can't tell if he's dreaming or not, or if I've crossed over to his world or we've met somewhere in between. But it seems to be the words of his song that has summoned him, much the way that Traveler would sing to me to bring me to her.

"I'm starting to remember now," he says. "Who is she?"

"My imaginary friend." Vic's face is pale-white.

"You may not remember this all when you wake up, Vic," I say. "But I want you to try. I want you to remember that she has taken my life. And that I am going to need your help to bring me back."

"How?"

"You're going to have to visit me here, Vic. You're going to have to stay over here more often so we can work together. You'll have to find some way. Or, maybe you can talk to Erica."

"What?"

"I can talk to Erica. We can plan through her. But you'll have to be here sometime."

I wish I could explain the look on Vic's face. "I remember you so clearly. So absolutely clearly. How did I forget? What is she, Abbie? Is she a monster?"

"You can see her however you like, Vic. But she has taken away my life. She's taken my chance to live. And I don't know if I deserve it or not, but you're my only chance to get it back."

Thirty-Four

The morning after visiting Abbie, I am ridiculously tired at school, and then I have to run off to work. It's a slow night, a Monday, and I am able to slack off a little on the hustle. I smile and make chit chat with the regulars and generally push my tiredness to the side during this time. But when 8pm rolls along, I feel spent and I am the first one on shift to take my 15 minute break.

I go outside to the patio, having left my green apron in the back so as not to be harassed by customers. I see Vic sitting out there, jotting words into a notebook.

"No work today?" I ask him.

"No," he says. "Have a seat. Too much happened last night. I called in."

"Too tired for work but not too tired to sit around the Starbucks?"

"I didn't say I was too tired," he replied. "I said that too much happened. There's a difference."

"Oh."

"I'm just making sense of things. I somehow feel like I'm being ripped in two."

"What do you mean, Vic?" I ask. "What happened last night?"

Vic lights a new cigarette. "I don't know you would understand, Erica. I don't think that *I* understand. I wish I could talk about it with you. I don't know if I can bring myself to talk about it."

"You can, Vic, you can."

There's a lost look in his eyes. "Just sit with me, Erica."

I sit by his side and watch him as he smokes and makes markings in his notebook. He is a strikingly handsome man. I feel like I know what he's thinking, somehow. Like maybe she got through to him, or he remembered her.

I've been reading whatever I can that might help me understand what is going on. I started with hitting the internet, but couldn't find anything relevant. Then I started reading religious texts about having souls lost or trapped. I read legends and ghost stories.

I read the works of Edgar Allen Poe. I read Bradbury's *Something Wicked this Way Comes*, and for that matter, *Macbeth*. I read every book on the market about astral projection, possession, spiritual mediums, channeling the dead, and making deals with the devil.

Of all the things I read, none of them could touch Abigail's story. They all stopped short of painting the picture of someone being lost in a world that doesn't exist. The closest that I've come to reaching a better understanding of Abigail's plight was when I read the myth of Orpheus.

Orpheus was the greatest singer that there ever

was (I'm guessing he didn't meet Traveler). He moved everything around him with deep emotions when he played his harp and sang his words. The trees uprooted themselves to get closer to his singing. And, of course, he married a beautiful woman who he was very in love with.

But happy endings don't exist in the Bronze Age. Orpheus' wife died and went to Hades, a very prized possession.

Orpheus wanted her back, so he traveled to Hell, trying to retrieve her. He sang his song and the Ferryman was moved and took him across the River Styx. When he finally played for the God of the Dead, Hades was so moved that he released his wife to him, on the condition that he never look back until the two of them were to the surface, back to the world of people.

Like I said, there are no happy endings here. Like the fool that he is, he looks back at his wife at the last possible moment—just in time to see her fade away forever.

Last time I visited Abigail, that story was heavy in my head. Orpheus' singing, I'm sure, couldn't touch that of Traveler's. And perhaps that was part of her power over Abigail.

Whatever the case, I stand afraid of Abigail fading away like Eurydice. Whatever I do, if we get close to getting her, I don't want to look back.

My watch beeps and I see that my 15 is over. I stand up to say goodbye to Vic. Vic stands up and gives me a tight hug. As we separate, he looks into my eyes. I hug him again, sorry for the knowledge that he doesn't have.

"Erica," he says. "Abigail told me I could talk to you. Is that right?"

I can't believe my ears.

"Can I?"

"I have to get back to work, Vic. You have some time tonight?"

Thirty-Five

I sit up in bed, talking to Tydomin who is lying on her sleeping bag on the ground.

"Tell me about the future, Ty."

"What do you want to know?" she says.

"Tell me how we save Abigail. You've already said that it's on Halloween. But that's a long time away. How do we do it?"

Tydomin is silent for a while. I can see that she is staring up at the ceiling, and her eyes have become very narrow in thought.

"I don't think I said that, Erica."

"Yes you did, Ty. You said that Traveler would be vulnerable on Halloween."

Tydomin looks very confused. "It's very hard to see, Erica. I've never tried to see between worlds like this. But I can tell you that I never said that you win this thing. I've never said that Traveler would be 'vulnerable.' I don't know how it's supposed to work, but things will be ripe at Halloween. I never said you'd save Abbie then."

"What do you mean, ripe?"

"I can't put my finger on it. But they're not ready

yet. Traveler and Abigail aren't ready to go back yet. And did you see the look on Vic's face when he was here? He's not ready. He says he is because those are the right words. But, I mean, you saw he isn't. I hate to have to withhold details." Tydomin sits up on her sleeping bag. "I'm sorry, Erica. I can't tell you if you save Abigail or not. It's not my job to tell you what happens."

"Tydomin, if that's not your job, then what is?"

Tydomin looks at me very seriously. "You haven't understood me from the beginning," she says.

"You're supposed to tell me what's going to happen, how we can defeat her."

"No," she says. "I'm supposed to *see* what happens, and give you advice based on that. There is a big difference. And I've told you that you should be patient. And I've told you that she used something that she keeps in the other world to get to where she is. But I never told you that you will win. I can't tell you that."

"Why?"

"For one, I will never tell you what happens. Well, that's the closest I'll ever come to telling you what happens. I read the situation and make recommendations. I've told you when the time will be ripe. It's up to you if you act on that or not."

"Well," I say. "Do we act on that?"

Tydomin's eyes get wide in a questioning gesture. "That's up to you, remember? I'm not about to *tell* you what happens. That leads to second guessing. It alters everything to tell someone."

"But *you* know."

"Yes. Well, I know more than I'm telling you, I suppose."

"God, do we have to play this game? Where I ask the just-right questions? Do you play a role in it?"

"I'm playing a role now. It's up to you if you keep me in it or not."

"Oh," I throw up my hands in frustration. "What questions can I ask you, Tydomin?"

"Oh, I know how to explain it! Think of a tarot deck," she says. "You told me that a tarot deck doesn't work to tell you the future, but works to tell you the influences."

"That's not fair, Tydomin. We asked you to help us, not to hide information from us."

"In what way do you want me to help you? By telling you the way your struggle will end up? That discredits a struggle, Erica. Trust me. You wouldn't feel right. And if I tell you that you don't succeed, you won't feel right about not waging the fight. It's a lose-lose situation. If you knew you'd win, you might not struggle. If you don't struggle, you can't do hard things."

This comment makes me think. Maybe it's true what the Buddhists say, that the goal is the path. If we live our lives by our code, and we struggle by our code, then what does it matter what the outcome is? We will still have our integrity.

"I've told you what I can about the history of the changeling. That at least lets you know, somewhat, of what you're up against. You know you're not crazy, and that should be some reassurance. And I've told you that there's something in her world that Abbie can use to help you. Now it's your turn to struggle, so you can either win, or be better next time you have to do something hard."

"Just tell me this, Tydomin: is it possible to beat her?"

Tydomin eases her posture and slumps down a little, so longer trying to defend herself. "Your words, Erica, this is too much. You are asking specific information about how the future will end up. If you knew the answer to this was 'no,' would you still follow through and *try* to beat her? I can't do anything that would risk you changing your mind."

I try to think of a better way to put it. "When will be the best time to initiate our plan?"

"What is your plan?"

"To break the spell."

"How?"

And to this I am speechless. I imagined that we would just get Abbie to seduce her into trading places, the same way she had been seduced. But it had been months already and it was apparent that Abbie couldn't exert influence on Traveler, and was unable to initiate contact with her.

"How," Tydomin says, "is the crux of the whole thing. How do you reverse a spell?"

"Usually the person who casts the spell has to reverse it," I answer. "But in this case, I just don't know how to get her to do it."

"Get *who* to do it?"

"Tydomin, I have to get -" And then it hits me.

"This spell took two people to cast." I sit and I think. I can see that there's a smile on Tydomin's face. "I need more help, Tydomin. I'm close. I need more help."

"Oh, come on now, Erica. There's got to be someone under the stars that can help you."

Thirty-Six

I draw my circle with my dagger. I draw my circle with my wand. I light the candles. I wrap myself in my star blanket. I beg to the Goddess: "Great Goddess, giver of birth to all things, guide me tonight." In each hand I hold a polished and pointed amethyst. I kneel on the ground, in the center of my pentagram, and quiet my mind. I listen only to my breathing, like Abbie taught me. I see the energy of the new breath as it comes in, and I feel the release of the used up, old breath as it goes out.

The star blanket absorbs me again, like during my vision quest. I feel once again like I am at one with the world. I have garbled visions too overwhelming to maintain, a bird's eye view of my life. At last, I am standing once again on top of the mountain with my grandmother. My grandmother is laughing, and I am terribly troubled.

"What is it, child, that bothers you so much?"

"Grandmother, I'm afraid my friend may be lost. I don't know how to help her."

"You cannot help her anymore," my grandmother laughs.

"Grandmother, she cannot be lost forever," I say. "The seer child pointed me to you. She said that you can help me find a way to bring her back."

Off in the distance, clouds are gathering. It's going to be a stormy night on the mountain, and I don't want to be here for it. I become frightened, and I'm not sure why. I have the urge to take the star blanket off of me, and to give up on Abbie.

"Come over here, Erica. Come here and let me look at you," my grandmother says. "I am here to tell you to let go of your guilt. It's not your fault that you haven't been able to save Abigail. It's not your job to save her."

"What do you mean? If not me then who?"

My grandmother has a soft smile on her face. She is beautiful to look at. "Your friend, Abbie, has known how she can be saved all along. You struggle for your own conscience now. Let it be clear."

In the distance, a lightning bolt strikes. The thunder rolls over to us and knocks me down. I am suddenly on the floor, in the middle of the pentagram, wrapped up in my blanket. I stand up and roll the blanket up. I grab my recorder, redraw the circle, and get ready to project. It's time to talk to Abbie.

Thirty-Seven

Tonight, Traveler is lying here and I have already tried every way to wake her up. I feel like, if I can just talk to her, I won't worry so much anymore. I can be okay with this, if I can just let her know how not okay with it I am.

Then, I see Erica fly through the window. She perches on the bed, once again.

"Abbie," she yells. "You know how to break the spell?"

"You shouldn't be here, Erica. What if Traveler wakes up?"

"She's not waking up, Abbie. You've been doing this for months and months. She's not waking up. Samhain is fast approaching, and we don't have a lot of time to prepare. How do we break the spell?"

I don't know how Erica found out. "Erica," I say. "I don't deserve to break the spell."

"What are you talking about?"

"I don't deserve it. Do you remember when I told you about the banishing list? Do you remember that I tried to banish *you* because I was frightened of what you meant to me? I tried to banish Teri because I resented her. I tried to banish Vic, because he was my weakness. I wanted to banish my situation, because it made me depressed. And I wanted to banish my own mother, because of the pain she caused me by dying."

"You wanted to banish those *attributes* from yourself."

"What's the difference? Those things are what make up life, Erica. I wanted to banish my very *life*. That's what I did. I banished my life. That's why I'm here."

Erica, who is no longer a bird, but her physical self, looks angry. "You can't leave us behind. You can't leave us with this bitch in your place. What do we do to fix this?"

I roll my eyes at her. I don't have to tell her, but I will. It doesn't make any difference, if I don't choose to go through with it. "I have Traveler's grimmerie. I don't know how she brought it here, but she did. It's strange; it's not like it's written in a language. It's like I open the book and I just *understand* it, you know? It tells me how to break the spell. There's a pretty simple, but she has to be tricked. It will be much easier if it's on Samhain because the veil will be thin. We won't have to fight her as hard."

"But how?"

"She has to sing, and she has to hold still in a holy circle drawn by a witch for a few minutes. I can play her instrument on this side and come out on that side. But she has to sing long enough and not stop before it's too late. That's the hard part."

"Abbie, you really need to listen to me. Vic is

ready to help. I'm ready to help. We've just been waiting on the timing, and a plan. The time is right, now, and I just found out that you have a plan! Maybe we can get Vic to get Traveler to sing."

"I've thought of that," she says. "I think the chance of it working is pretty small."

"Then there's hope?"

"For what, Erica?"

"For you, Abbie. Don't give up on this; we can do it. We can get you back, Abbie."

"I just don't know, Erica. I think that maybe my turn is over."

Erica closes her eyes tightly. "Abbie," she says. "You're right, Samhain is coming up. For whatever reason, the seer thinks that the time will be ripe then. I believe her. You have to make up your mind, and you have to help us. I want you back."

And I can't decide. I can't decide if I deserve it or not.

Thirty-Eight

It must be Samhain. I have no real sense of time, but I can tell that it's Samahin, because even though the room is empty, and no one is around to light the room with their life, I can see the room a little. It's dim and it's dark, but I can make out features of the room. I search the room to make sure there's no one here, and there isn't. During Samhain, the veil between worlds is at its thinnest. I am close to the real world. I feel just a little bit more myself, and I remember just a little bit what it was like to be me.

"Sweetheart," I hear called out in the darkness. The sound, so very close to being an audio sensation in the world of mossy darkness, startles me. It is the voice of my mother, I recognize right away.

"Mom?" I call out.

"It's me, Abbie. I'm holding your hand. Can you not see me?"

"No, Mom, I can't."

"I was afraid of that," she says. I am kept such wonderful company by her voice that I feel like I could cry and cry forever out of happiness.

"I wish I could see you," I say. "Do you have any

idea what's happened to me?"

The warm voice returns, "I've been watching you, when I could, Abbie. I should have told you about your sister earlier."

I hold and feel her hand. It touches my face, and I become aware of my face for the first time since I've been in this state.

"We have some time, honey," my mother says. "So I will tell you the whole story. I only wish I had told you earlier."

"You know about Traveler?"

In the dark room, my mom starts to tell me her story.

Thirty-Nine

I was eleven years old when it happened, she says.

I grew up in a beautiful house on maybe the most beautiful street in the world. There were a few kids in the neighborhood that I played with, when I wasn't going off to deliveries with my mother. We were always talking about the man who lived in the house behind us. Our parents all called him the musician, since he had moved there from Germany to design and build a pipe organ in a local church. He had been working on it since the end of the Second World War, but still wasn't finished. The story was that after the organ had been installed, he insisted on carving, by hand, all the woodwork around the instrument. The kids on the street and I all misinterpreted this and called him the magician. He was old with a long white beard, and we were all a little scared of him.

From my bedroom, I could hear him playing the piano, or his small organ, when he wasn't at work in the church. I would light incense and sit with a book and listen to him play for hours. One day, when my mother was gone to a birth, and Dad was at his job at the language institute, I sat and listened to him play.

He stopped playing and I could see him leave his house to go back to the church with his tools strapped together under his arm.

Feeling lonely in the house, I walked down to the ocean, just a couple of blocks. I had done it with friends and by myself millions of times. Pacific Grove had never known any crime; there was no reason for my parents to forbid me to do it.

I sat on a rock and watched the ocean. It was a clear and sunny day, and I had nothing in mind but to sit there for a while and look for whales and porpoises crossing the bay over the underwater canyon. Not seeing any, I climbed down the rocks and walked along the small sandy beach looking for shells. The beach was only there at low tide, so I didn't get much of a chance to collect shells.

I walked down the beach, putting the rocks in my pocket. I was startled by a sound behind me and I turned around to see a man in a service uniform standing behind me.

"Hello, little girl," he said. "Where are your parents?"

"At work," I said, naively.

"Really," he said. "Would you like to see something?"

And my god, Abbie. He grabbed me.

I was scared, and I kicked him and broke his hold. I turned to run. Where we were was far down below the road, and I could never have climbed the rocks up. But I sprang for them anyway, since I knew that was the only way to get anyone's attention.

He grabbed me when I was half-way up the first small stone. He pulled me to the ground and covered my mouth. I was staring at the rocks that the waves were breaking on, and it was like they turned into a forest of rocks and waves surrounding me. Like I left my body and hid in the rocks while he had a hold on me.

When he was done with me, he wrapped his hands around my throat and squeezed and squeezed. I was back in my body to see his face and feel the world shatter in my throat. The world faded away from me, and I was grateful for it. When I woke up, I was in a hospital room with my parents around me. I couldn't speak for a while, didn't want to eat.

I got better, but I couldn't sleep after that. I mean, I couldn't sleep at all. Every time I shut my eyes in a dark room, I heard myself screaming. It was as real as anything. I saw his face in front of me. I felt him on top of me. I could feel his hands around my neck. I screamed and screamed all night long, no matter how my mother tried to help.

I couldn't look at the ocean, at the beach. The rocks that felt like they were protecting my mind were now ominous and frightening. I couldn't stand the thought of the ocean.

She cast spell after spell and had ritual after ritual to try and rid me of the horror that I went through every single day. I was in therapy and seeing a medical doctor regularly. It was their opinion that I couldn't physically last much longer like this.

It was a Sunday, I think, and I was sitting in the

parlor with my parents. Mom was reading a book to me, and I was trying not to fall asleep. There was a knock at the door. Mom and Dad were surprised to see that it was the musician.

"Good day," he said, very formally. "I hope that you don't mind that I bring a gift for your daughter." He had heard, of course, about the crime. There had never been anything else like it in that small town up until then. And he had heard my cries from his house day after day.

He invited us to our front porch, where he had the gift. It was the bed you are laying on right now, Abigail.

"I was saving this wood for a piano," he told them. "It is very special wood that I've had since I was a much younger man. But I think that your daughter can use it more."

My parents thanked him for the very kind gesture.

"I know it seems simplistic. But I think that this new bed may give your daughter some comfort."

"She's been sleeping with us," my mother said. "This is too fine of a gift for us to accept."

"No ma'am, it is not. Let your daughter decide if she wants the bed. After all, the gift is for her."

I walked up to the headboard and gazed at it for a while. The angels and the grain of the wood, and everything else about it seemed wonderful to me. I begged my parents to let me keep it.

We set the bed up in my room, but I didn't sleep on it yet. There was a new horror in my life. We discovered that I was pregnant. I had never had my period before. This child was the result of my very first ovulation. My family was devastated.

Abigail, I beg you not to judge me harshly in this matter. Don't judge your grandmother too harshly either. We were frightened women, and if it happened again, I don't know what to tell you that I would do. I just honestly don't know the truth. It is something that I am glad not to know.

Mom made me a very strong tea. It tasted awful.

"It's made with Silphium," she told me. "Silphium is thought to be extinct. But, it is the privilege of very few witches to be the custodians of it. It is a very powerful herb. And it will rid you of this man's child."

My mother said that she sensed evil in the child. Dad insisted that we get rid of it. I didn't want to bear the burden of it either. And I probably felt very close to how you feel right now; I was very nearly out of my mind.

And just like Mom said, the baby was lost.

For some reason, that night, I decided to sleep in the bed that the magician gave to me. I felt like I should leave my parents' room, despite the fact that Mom wanted to force me to stay in there so she could keep an eye on me.

That was the first night I ever saw Traveler.

Traveler told me that she was my daughter. She didn't blame me for what I had done, but she was instead very excited to see me and to have me with her. I kept her secret, of course, but I always enjoyed spending time with this very little girl who seemed to know so much. She was confident that when I was ready, I would have another child and that she would be it. Until then, she said, she wanted to get to know me as much as possible.

My family left Pacific Grove just a couple months after that. We wanted to leave it behind us, and we swore we'd never go back. I never wanted to see the coast again. My dad found a job here and Mom started practicing midwifery here.

As I got older, so did Traveler. In fact, she got older much faster than I did. And as she got older, she started showing me more and more about witchcraft. She taught me spells and recipes for teas and incense and so much more. Mom was amazed at what I was coming up with in my practice.

When I met your father, and I got pregnant with you, Traveler was thrilled. I only saw her once in a while, of course, in dreaming when I would visit the bed. And when you were born, Traveler was heartbroken. She didn't understand how it could be that she wasn't my daughter. She had been so positive of it.

She got a little mean after that. Just generally snotty and angry, especially when she found out that I would never be able to conceive again. I stopped visiting her after that, and did my best to forget everything about her. Which was very easy to do. She was in such a distant world that without regular interaction, all memory of that world disappears.

I put the bed in your room when you were old

enough for it, convinced that Traveler had been nothing but an imaginary friend that I had created to help me get through that terrible trauma. Had I known any better, I would have burned the bed before giving it to you.

Forty

Mom whispered her story to me in the dark.

"Did she have anything to do with you dying?" I ask her. "You did die on this bed."

"I've wondered, since I died, if my brain condition was a spell, or a botched spell, of hers. If she had tried to do something to get into me and ended up doing enough just to make me so sick."

"But," I say. "You slept on the bed those last few weeks. Did you see her then?"

"I can't remember, Abbie," she says. "I don't remember much about that time. I was wasting away so fast. I'm suspicious, that's all I can say."

"But what does this make me?"

Mom was quiet for a moment, holding my hands in hers. "I'm not sure," she says. "Some kind of inorganic being, I suppose. Something that can perceive life. That's why Traveler and your friend Erica seem to glow and illuminate the world around them when they're near. We must have looked that way to Traveler, beacons of light in a lifeless world. She must have been so jealous of our life forces.

"Whatever the case," my mother continues, "we need to get you back to the world. She doesn't belong here."

"I don't know if I belong there, anymore."

"Abigail," I felt my mom's arms wrap around me. "You belong. You are the only part of me left in the world. I want you to come back. I know that you know how. Tell Erica."

"But it's too late," I say. "It's Samhain, isn't it?"

"Abbie, that's tomorrow night. We're close to it, but if it was Samhain, you could see me clearly, I'm fairly sure."

I feel tears in my eyes, even though I don't have eyes. I feel my mom wrap her arms around me, even though there is no me there.

Forty-One

I'm a witch. Whatever you think about that doesn't matter to me. Whatever connotations you have with the word, keep them to yourself. Whatever of my story you believe, keep that to yourself too. As a witch, I've lived by a code, I've followed the path. I've harmed no one. I've trusted my decisions. I've been true to myself. I've loved the Earth and the Goddess and I've loved all they've created.

But I stand here in darkness, on the night that the veil between worlds at its thinnest. I know that it's Samhain, because even though I don't exist right now, my blood tells me it is. My nature tells me it's time to renew. It's time to banish what I haven't liked about my life in the last year.

Everything depends on our plan.

Erica comes through the window, solid, human, and not a part of my lonely world. She has used a ladder to climb up to the roof and the window was left unlocked by Vic last night. She looks at the bed and whispers, "Hi, Abigail. Wish us all luck." Erica rushes to the vanity and drops a small pile of cone incense out of her pocket onto the top of the vanity. Then she pulls out her dagger and starts to call upon the Goddess to keep her us safe within the circle of this room.

Her incantation is not yet finished when we hear voices coming up the stairs. It's Vic and Traveler coming home from a Halloween party. Erica cannot rush her work, as she must make sure that the circle and complete and blessed. The voices are right outside the door when she finishes and rushes to hide under the bed. I can hear her trying to quiet her breathing when the door bursts open.

Vic is dressed up like a pirate: the only costume I've ever seen him wear in all the years I've known him. Traveler is dressed as the caricature of a witch—a conical hat, broomstick, striped socks—but an exceedingly sexy version. They laugh. I suspect they have had too much to drink. When they laugh, they shine more brightly.

I told Erica about my conversation with Mom. I told her what to do to help me. I told Vic last night that the time was ready. I told him what he had to do. And the three of us are nervous that the slightest error in timing will let Traveler know what we are planning.

And I'm just a little worried, after seeing their love-making so many times, that Vic does not want to banish Traveler.

I know the counter-spell in the grimmerie by heart now. Erica knows it by heart now. Vic knows his by heart now.

Traveler starts kissing Vic. Her boyfriend.

I draw my circle. I draw it where I drew it last year. Where Erica drew hers moments ago.

"Let's light some incense," Vic says, breaking their kiss. And he fishes for the incense that Erica left on the vanity when she entered the room, hoping Traveler doesn't notice.

I beg for the help and wisdom of the Great Earth Goddess tonight. I beg for my own forgiveness.

"Traveler," Vic says. "I want you to sing for me."

"Later," she says, reaching for him.

"No, Traveler, now. I have an idea for a song. I want you there with me, on stage. I want your voice to ring out with my instrument."

Traveler smiles. She stands there in the middle of the room and removes Vic's silly looking pirate hat. She kisses him again, rubbing his arms. Vic kisses her back and I keep thinking, *come on, we don't have all day!*

"Sing," Vic says. "I want to watch you. I want you to stand there," Vic sits down on a chair next to the vanity. "I want you to sing, just for me. I want to hear your voice. I want to listen and be your captive audience."

"What shall I sing?" She sways a little, looking drunk.

"One of those songs you sing, where it's not like words, but just your full voice. Take a few minutes. I'll play with you, just follow my chords." Vic picks up the acoustic guitar that he has been keeping in her closet so that he can play while visiting. He plays through a chord progression. "Like that, at first," he says. "Can you keep up?"

She sings. And she sings and their music together is nothing less than beautiful. Her voice wanders the room; his guitar fills in around it. The two of them have chemistry and the music sounds so moving, so emotional. I had no idea that a ballad could break one's heart so fully.

They play for five minutes or so, and Vic changes the chord progression, moving it just a little and Traveler senses this and follows at just the right time. It's a spell binding musical experience and I don't think it's just because of where I am that I feel so profoundly moved.

Then the chords drop a little. The music moves lower and Traveler follows.

"Now," Vic says quietly with what looks like tears in his eyes. And he moves it lower still and she follows lower, and at this time I pick up the small, strange flute and play along. We make a harmony that moves again with Vic's guitar, and moves again lower, and it's almost a shame that I'm the only one that can hear all three of us playing together.

Traveler falls to her knees, but keeps singing. "It's beautiful, Traveler," Vic calls out. "Lower, my love, lower. I want to hear your voice ring."

Traveler sings, her voice falling. She holds her stomach. I play with her, lower.

I hear a gasp from under the bed. Erica is surprised to suddenly see Traveler fading from view, while, at the same time, the bed suddenly registers a slight amount of my weight, as Traveler and I begin to cross worlds.

Suddenly, Traveler stops singing. "What are you doing to me, Vic?"

"Keep singing, Traveler, please. Don't make this last, Traveler."

Traveler suddenly is looking right at me. "No, Abbie. You need to stop right now. Stop him, stop yourself. It's my turn, Abbie! It's still my turn! You've had your turn!"

"You know?" Vic says, still playing.

"What do you take me for?" Traveler is in tears. Her voice cracks under her sobbing. "Of course I knew. How did *you* know?"

"Now," I say, and Vic and Erica hear me. Vic moves the music up, I join the music, I become more solid. It's too late for Traveler. She jumps at me, but she is intercepted by Erica.

Erica comes out from under the bed and stands between my sister and me. She holds a dagger at the fading girl and says, "The Goddess commands you to stay still." She is deep within her circle, the one that she drew, and Traveler has no power there.

But Traveler laughs. "She's no witch," she says. If she's talking to me, Vic, or The Goddess, I can't tell. Her face goes from something resembling fear to the sharp ugliness of anger. "You're no witch. You two are nothing. You're not my sister," she spits in my direction. "You are *nothing* to me."

"Traveler," I say loudly to get her attention. "Mother and I always loved you. But it's not your world. Now can we stop this? Can we go back to how we were?"

She moans and wails like frightened animal.

I play the instrument. I raise the note. I

concentrate.

I don't feel pressure or pain, like you might feel when you are born. But I can feel myself becoming heavier. I can feel myself becoming real. And I can see the look or horror on Traveler's face, as she diminishes. I can feel the bed release me, and I can feel the essence of my big sister pass into the bed.

The look on Vic's face is a mix of amazement and sorrow. He keeps playing guitar until I am solid.

I feel heavy. I am covered in sweat. Things sound different; they sound alive. I can hear the life in Erica's voice as she rushes over to hold me, to ask if I'm okay, to ask if it's done. I can hear the last notes ring in the body of Vic's guitar as he sets it down and comes over to give me a hug.

The world is bright. The lights are out and only the moonlight shines through the window, but even that seems overwhelming.

The touch of skin is electric. Erica's fingers and her face against mine feel vibrant and solid. Vic's hand on the back of my head feels stable and secure.

Erica holds me on the floor next to the bed while the two of us start crying, tears of joy and sadness. Vic steps out the window to have a smoke, leaning up against the house.

"You're here, you're alive," Erica says over and over. She rubs me and holds me close. She keeps drawing my scent in, holding it in.

I watch out the window at the smoke dissipating from Vic's cigarette in the moonlight.

I can't help but to wonder what he is thinking.

Forty-Two

Erica breaks the silence of our car ride. "I can't believe you're doing this."

"Why not?"

"There's so much that we can learn, Abbie."

Vic is driving his dad's truck. But he hasn't said so much as a word since we loaded the back of the truck with my bed and several other items from my room. Erica and I sit in the back of the crew cab, holding each other's hands, hoping that the touch will anchor me to this world again.

"I don't want to learn any more from her," I say.

"But we have control now. We have the power. We can ask her things, we can study her. Gods, Abbie, we don't even know the first thing about that world that you were locked in for so long. How long was it? Ten months of your life?"

I look past Erica at the valley below fading into the fog. "I know enough about it, Erica. And I know that Traveler isn't someone that you get power over. We got lucky. She has to be destroyed."

Vic doesn't add anything. He hasn't said much to me. I don't think he can handle any of this. He never asked to be part of it, after all.

"I just think it's a mistake. I think we can do better. We have a chance to do so much with this."

"Why, Erica? For power? For personal power? It's not worth it. And it's no one's choice but mine."

"You're right about that," Erica says.

In silence, we carry the parts of the bed to the fire pit.

"Is that all of it?" I ask Erica.

"That's all," Erica says. "That's all."

"Are you sure."

"Abbie, that's the bed, right there."

I dowse the wood with gasoline. I throw on a match. I watch as the smoke bleeds up into the sky. I watch as it disperses and is carried off by the wind. I feel it as it curls and bends in the currents of the atmosphere.

Part of me is going up in smoke.

Erica leaves me to watch the fire by myself, in a solemn ceremony. I watch as my mother's bed burns. I once heard that the fire that comes out of wood when it is burned is the sunlight that the tree collected over its life. It is the energy it gathered being released back into the universe.

"Are you *sure*?" Erica's voice still rings in my ears.

I burn the bed. I watch it release its collected sunlight into the universe.

I burn my wand.

I burn a bag with my incense, my oils, my potion ingredients. I watch them release their energy.

I burn my family's grimmerie. And it puts a lump in my throat.

I burn my flute.

Erica asked me why I have to get rid of all of this stuff. She asked me if I was still Wiccan. She asked me if I was still a witch.

I told her I wasn't sure. But that I had been in the mysterious dark side of life, and didn't have the faith that light would rise again. "If I am going to be a witch, if I *am* a witch, I have to do it on my own terms," I told her. "It can't be built on this foundation. I can't carry my baggage and my mother's baggage around with me." It was true, what I told her. That if I was going to return to the craft, it would have to grow from a seed. It is part of the bargain that I made for myself when I decided to take my life back. I decided that I had to re-grow it. I let go of my life not because a monster came out and took it, but because I didn't feel like I fit it anymore. I know in my heart that she couldn't have taken me if I had felt at peace. She couldn't have taken me if I hadn't offered myself to Vic for nothing in return; if I had owned up and been responsible for my feelings for Erica; if I didn't run in fear from my father's relationship; none of this would have happened.

I want a life I can fit in. I want to grow a new one. If I am to be a witch, I will welcome it. And if I am not to be one, I will mourn the loss. But it will be *my* direction.

I look down the road, where Erica and Vic wait for me. I have to sow their seeds back into my life, too.

The first night I was back, Erica stayed with me, holding me all night. She said that she would be overwhelmed. She wouldn't know what to do if she had lost so many months. If she had to burn her religion. If she had to choose between Erica and Vic or possible neither of them.

I'm not overwhelmed.

Erica, Vic, music, school, witchcraft, Dad, Teri, Mom. I don't know what role they play in my life anymore.

Life is an exciting mystery.

The tapestry of possibilities that surround me is rich and wonderful. I can't wait to find out what's in store.

The End.

ABOUT THE AUTHOR

Sol Smith is a writer and writing professor. He lives in California with his wife, four children, and two very awkward dogs. He has nine books in publication, including *California Dreadfuls*, a childrens horror series, and the blockbuster hit, *Travels With Charlie: A Modern Search for America.*